OTHER BOOKS BY CATHERINE LANE

The Set Piece
Heartwood

OTHER BOOKS IN
THE WINDOW SHOPPING COLLECTION

Tread Lightly by Catherine Lane (Book One)

Coming 2017:
A Work in Progress by L. T. Smith
The Last First Time by Andrea Bramhall
Party Wall by Cheyenne Blue

CATHERINE LANE

TREAD LIGHTLY

ACKNOWLEDGMENTS

Many thanks to Ylva Publishing and Astrid Ohletz, who asked me to be part of the *Window Shopping* project.

To Susan X Meagher, who talked me off the ledge when I was ready to throw *Tread Lightly* into the digital trash can.

To Ann Etter and Ameliah Faith, who dropped everything for quick beta reads.

To JoSelle Vanderhooft and Alissa McGowan, who made so many excellent suggestions.

And finally to Sandra Gerth, who is always willing to go the extra mile to make me better. I am very grateful.

To my wife, who always believed in the story...and in me.

CHAPTER 1

Present

THE SUN REFLECTED OFF THE window, obscuring the view of the shop inside. Still, Claire was hyperaware of the products on display. She shuffled her feet and coughed but didn't move toward the door. In the window, she caught the reflection of Tamiel's easy smile, as if she frequented sex toy stores all the time.

"You're kidding. Right?" The guardian angel shimmered in the sunlight as she chuckled. "It's in there?"

"The magic calls to you. You don't get to choose." Claire bit her bottom lip.

"It has a very interesting sense of humor," Tamiel said.

"I'll say."

Tamiel rubbed her hands. "Okay. So let's go get it."

As if it were that easy. Claire closed her eyes, blocking out the mannequins dressed in leather teddies. A powerful force churned around her. It reached out from the store like a tidal wave, swirling around her body and then yanking her forward. She had to dig her heels into the sidewalk to stay upright.

The magic was raw, not filtered and refined the way the Fairy Godmother Council delivered it. Another surge tugged at her, and immense power coursed around her again, almost pulling her under. Panic flared. She had been around magic all her life, but it had never been this demanding or potent.

She reached out for Tamiel, and the angel's hand was instantly under her arm, steadying her.

"Can you do this?" Tamiel asked softly, no longer teasing.

"I don't know," Claire said. "I... I'm not sure I can control it."

As if sensing her hesitation, the magic yanked her forward, smashing her shin into the bottom edge of the display window. Metal cracked against bone, and for the second time in three days, a sharp pain shot up her leg.

"Son of a..."

CHAPTER 2

Three Days Earlier

"...BANSHEE!" CLAIRE CRIED.

The coffee table had come out of nowhere and slammed into her shin. She hopped around the small living room, howling like a cat in heat and holding her leg. A glance down told her what she already knew. Blood trickled down her lower leg and pooled in the tip of her blue slipper.

What an idiot. No, worse. She had been so concerned about closing this case fast that she had rushed her entry. And now Claire—fairy godmother: level-one-plus, the golden child of the Fairy Godmother Council—looked like a newbie.

The young woman, her client, had been reading a magazine on the couch but had leaped up when Claire materialized right in front of her. Her eyes, first round with surprise, had narrowed into a hard glare almost immediately.

"Who the hell are you?" She rolled the magazine into a stiff tube and waved it in Claire's direction. "How did you get in here?"

"Relax, Jenna." Shit, that wasn't right. Jenna was last week's case. This girl pulsating with hostility was named... Claire brought the top sheet of case number 69317 into focus in her mind. That's right. It was Abigail—Abby for short?

"Relax, Abby." She took a shot.

Neither Abigail nor Abby backed down. Instead, she danced on the balls of her feet and jabbed the magazine across the coffee table. "Get the hell out of here. I took a self-defense course. I know how to use this."

"Yes. I'm sure you do. But put it down and listen to me." Claire dropped her foot to the ground. She held it there even as a sharp pain shot up her leg. She needed to look the part and, frankly, put a little magic back into the moment.

She forced a smile to her lips and hoped the incarnation she had chosen—a short, plump woman dressed in blue silks and a pointy cap—would do the trick. At the moment, she was a carbon copy of the fairy godmother from the live-action remake of *Sleeping Beauty* currently streaming online. Of course, this frumpy version didn't resemble what she'd looked like when she had actually appeared to Princess Aurora back when she'd been an apprentice, level-ten-minus, but this day and age left no room for subtlety.

"Guess what?" Claire threw her hands in the air. "I'm your fairy godmother!"

"Don't come any closer, you crazy-ass freak." Again, the girl jabbed the magazine at her. "Are you looking for Todd? He's selling whatever your DOC is in two-twelve. This is two-ten."

"DOC?"

"Drug of choice."

"No. I'm not looking for drugs." Claire shook her head. It had been such an easy case on paper. That happy scenario had disintegrated the minute she slammed into the coffee table. She took a deep breath, tamped down the pain still shooting up her leg, and studied the girl in front of her. Shoulder-length, brown hair framed an angular face. Metal piercings ran all the way down her left ear and jumped over to her nose and eyebrow. Abby stood frozen, her brown eyes two tiny pinpoints of resentment and anger.

Yep, things had definitely changed over the centuries. Sleeping Beauty and this young woman were barely the same species.

"Get out, or I'm calling the cops." Abby's hand darted for her cell phone on the coffee table.

Claire pulled her wand, Carothann, from the invisible pocket of magic that always rode at her hip. One flick and the cell phone ricocheted across the glass top before Abby's fingers could get there.

"What the hell?" She looked up at Claire for an explanation.

Claire waved the slender rowan branch with a theatrical flourish and sent her intentions straight to its core. The wand, trembling in her hand, strained ever so slightly, and magic filled the room.

Invisible trumpets blew a soft fanfare, and a gentle wind lifted her blue cape. Golden dust shot up into the air.

As the golden shimmer settled over them both, the hardened look faded from Abby's eyes. Claire couldn't suppress her grin. The power of magic worked every time. She had her now. Thank goodness.

Abby laughed with a loud hoot. "Oh my God! I'm on *Punk Me*. Right?" She dropped the magazine on the coffee table with a clunk and spun about the room. "Where's the camera? Is Van Woods here? Oh my God, he is so cute."

"Abby, concentrate." She snapped her wand against the air. "Fairy. God. Mother." Golden sparks like tiny fireworks shot out of Carothann's tip with every word.

Abby pursed her lips as she watched the sparklers fall to the ground. "I'm not being punked?"

"No."

"And you are?"

"Your fairy godmother. Level-one-plus."

Claire rocked back on her heels, in part to take weight off her still-aching leg, but mostly to give Abby time to let her unbelievable good fortune sink in. She waited for the tears of happiness, the squeals of delight, the—

"No thanks." Abby shook her head. "I don't need a fairy godmother. I'm okay."

"Seriously?" Claire glanced around the squalid studio apartment. Cockroaches skittered along the wall of the kitchenette. The furniture could have easily been found on a curb the day before.

The hardened look was back. "Yep."

"Listen to me. There're lots of different kinds of okay. I can offer you the happily-ever-after kind."

"Whatever." Abby threw up a hand in dismissal.

Claire forced another smile. Abby was pushing all her buttons. All her cases, lately, were about managing attitude first and creating new destinies second. She took a deep breath. "First step is to get you ready for the party. I'm afraid you're already very late."

"Party? What party?"

Claire clenched her teeth to keep the smile intact. "The annual sales party? At your company?"

"Oh yeah. That. I'm not going."

"But your Prince Charming is there. That's where you need to go if you're going to find a life that's more than just…okay." She waved Carothann around the room, pointing out a dark

6

stain on the carpet and then the oven door, which hung off one hinge.

"Office parties are lame. Especially on a Friday night." Abby rolled her eyes, as if just having to explain this fact was the largest imposition imaginable. "Besides, I have nothing to wear."

"I'm your fairy godmother, for goodness's sake."

"Yeah. I got that," she shot back. "And that's, like, relevant how?"

Crazy. If there wasn't a vampire or zombie involved, kids these days had no reference point.

Claire tightened her hold on Carothann. The wand felt warm and familiar in her hand, the only right thing in what was quickly becoming a difficult case. With a swift flick, she and the branch pulsated with power. She visualized what she wanted and the wand jumped to life. Golden tendrils of magic streaked to the far side of the room. A pile of paper napkins leaped to life in Abby's makeshift kitchen. They exploded into the air with a soft poof and floated back together to stitch an exact copy of the high-end dress on the cover of the magazine the girl had been reading.

"Oh my God!" Abby rushed to grab the masterpiece before it hit the floor. Her grin almost touched her eyes. Give her an expensive designer label, and she was all-in. Claire should have led with the dress.

"Shoes. I need shoes. Can they be Jimmy Choos?" Abby stroked the dress lovingly. "And, like, one of those cool, triple-choker necklaces all the rich girls have. I got to have one of those too."

Claire bit her lip and tried to push her annoyance back down into a place where she could ignore it. In the olden days, the makeover had been her absolute favorite part. Now it was a shopping frenzy, where the girls were like piranhas on steroids.

Still, Administration just wanted the case closed. A tick on the tally to show the magical world the FGC was still relevant in the twenty-first century.

Another flick of her wand and two *People* magazines hopped to attention on the coffee table. Rustling filled the air as their pages folded in on themselves and grew into metallic silver pumps. A second flick, and a used piece of dental floss in an ashtray squirmed into a sparkly necklace.

Abby scooped up her bounty. "Oh my God. I have Jimmy Choos."

"You know, it all vanishes at midnight."

"It does?"

"Yeah. You don't get to keep it."

"I don't?" Abby's face fell. "Not even the necklace?"

"Have you read even one fairy tale?"

Abby just stared at her.

"Those are the Council's rules. I didn't make them up."

"That totally sucks." Abby plopped onto the couch. "Seriously, I think—"

"All right, my dear. You'd better put it all on and get going."

Abby opened her mouth to start up again, but Claire jumped in first. "Chop-chop. Your ride is outside."

Claire pointed Carothann at a cockroach darting around the fridge. It instantly straightened up into a lanky man decked out in a chauffeur's hat and coat. Normally she would have chosen the more reliable spider in the opposite corner, but roaches were incredibly fast drivers, and Abby was getting later by the second.

The girl took forever to get ready, adjusting the straps on her dress and shoes again and again and putting product in her hair almost one strand at a time. So long that the chauffeur had dropped to the ground and tried to scuttle behind the couch. Claire was shooing the man back out into the open when her impatience boiled over.

"Abby! I can only put things in motion. You have to take it home yourself."

"Just a second," she said as she reached for her cell, still on the far side of the coffee table. Abby had snapped a selfie and was pulling up Snapchat.

"You've got to be kidding me." Carothann jumped in her hand, and the pictures winked out of existence.

Abby tapped the screen with a finger. "What'd you do?"

"Nothing permanent. It's frozen until after midnight. Just go to the party."

"I can't go without my phone." Huffing, she stamped her foot and held out her cell. "Fix it. I want a selfie."

How old was this girl? The file had said twenty-two, but with all this whining she was acting more like four. And that was being generous.

"No pictures. No exceptions." The Cottingley disaster of 1917 jumped to mind—when her idiot cousin Heloise had unbelievably popped up in photographs taken by two English girls. The FGC had moved heaven and earth to make the pictures read like fakes. And now, thanks to Heloise's indiscretion, a refresher workshop on photos and all social media was required once a year.

Claire plucked the phone from Abby's outstretched fingers and dropped it on the coffee table with a clatter and no comment. She then steered Abby to the chauffeur. His big ears twitched like the antennae they once were.

"Get her to the party." Claire patted the cockroach on the back and turned to Abby with one last warning. "And you must be home by midnight. Or all this—the dress, the shoes, the really nice Tesla outside—will disappear, and you will be the crazy woman walking around in napkins and *People* magazines and wearing dental floss around her neck."

Abby gave her a hard glare.

"Got it?"

"Give me my cell back. I'm not going until you do."

A tiny knot pulled tight in Claire's stomach. She needed to change tactics. Fast.

"Suit yourself." She shrugged and disappeared in a cloud of golden dust.

"Wait! Don't go." Panic rose in Abby's voice. "I'm sorry." Plaintive cries followed Claire all the way across town.

Celebrating a banner year, the employees of the Bluestone Paper Company were doing it up right. Streamers, balloons, and cut-out decorations had transformed the warehouse into a first-class party zone. A live band jammed on the loading dock, several barmen handed out free booze by the printing machines, and chefs with tall, puffy hats manned buffet tables in every corner. The longest line snaked out from the one where two men in kimonos were hand-rolling sushi.

Claire stood hidden from sight behind one of the industrial bookshelves in the back. She winced as her injured shin hit a heavy stack of paper on the shelf and wished she were brazen or stupid enough to dip into the magic stream to heal her leg. The FGC was very clear: no magic for personal use. Sure, everyone cheated a little, like taking a pen home from the office. But healing her leg would be like taking home the whole office. And somehow Upper Administration always knew.

Instead, her gaze zeroed in on the only human in the room who mattered—Bluestone's handsome star salesman. Abby's Prince Charming stood in line at the sushi table. He shifted his weight casually from foot to foot as he chatted happily with another male partygoer. He didn't seem to be in a hurry, but more tight knots formed in Claire's stomach. The hour hand of the big clock above the metal rolling doors was approaching ten. Just over two hours away from her firm midnight deadline. She knew Abby was on her way—the alarm in the girl's final plea told her that. She just needed to keep Charming out of trouble until she arrived.

The prince of Bluestone Paper stepped up to the table just as the sushi master slid a long caterpillar roll onto the serving plate. A step beyond an excellent appetizer, it was a work of art. Green avocado and bright red *masago* played like real scales on top of the roll, and two round pieces of octopus peered out like bug eyes on one end.

"Bravo," Charming said and led a round of applause. The sushi master bowed and waved an open hand over his creation. Charming, as well as everyone behind him, crowded the table to grab a piece.

Across the room, Claire gasped. Charming's fingers had not clasped eel and cucumber but a shapely hand that had snuck under his at the last instant. His gaze softened the moment it met the warm brown eyes that belonged to the hand's owner.

"Mother Chimera!" Claire drew out Carothann in a flash and pointed it at the pair, ready to flick Charming's sushi to the floor or push the woman back into the crowd—anything to break their connection and save him for Abby.

The wand was at its apex when she froze. A gentle smile played on the girl's lips as she stared back at the handsome man in front of her. The girl wasn't just pretty; sweetness and kindness, attributes that were undeniably absent in Abby, radiated off her.

Carothann dropped almost of its own accord. This was the true magic—love at first sight. No woman had looked at Claire like that for a very long time, but she hadn't forgotten how special it could be.

Mother of a manticore. Was she really thinking of letting them connect? It would break every rule in the FGC handbook. For sure, she would have to meet with Administration, and who knew what other punishments would follow?

But the pair clearly had the spark of true love. The whole room was staring at them. Abby, in all her petulance, would never generate anything close. True, he wasn't her client...but this happy ending would at least give the case some meaning it was sorely lacking. It might even put some purpose back in her own life. Besides, what could they do to her? She was a level-one-plus.

When Prince of Sales took Sushi Princess by the hand and led her onto the dance floor, Claire didn't strike him lame. When he leaned in and whispered in her ear, she didn't raise the volume of the band. Instead, she held Carothann tightly against her thigh. Already, a bright and shiny future was opening up around them. The edges of a new life were plainly visible to Claire, as if all the colors of the aurora borealis had drifted over them.

A perfect storybook ending. Except in this tale, Abby didn't make even one appearance, and Claire would, for the first time in her career, have an open case past her deadline.

The knots in her stomach tightened into one big heap. What the hell was she thinking? Yep, she would have a lot of explaining to do, and what was worse, she had brought it on herself.

Claire hesitated, her hand on the front door of the Fairy Godmother Council's Los Angeles branch. In the olden days, the offices had been called *keeps* and had been more about fun than work. Rooms in castles or great halls had been covered in rich tapestries, flowed with wine and food, and hosted all-day parties. But now, with the FGC on the verge of becoming obsolete, the Los Angeles office had been reduced to a small storefront in an abandoned mini-mall. A simple magic wash had made the outside so bare and uninviting that no unsuspecting human would dare drop in. Claire, hand still on the door, wished that she, too, could just walk past like the humans did. That knot in her stomach yanked even tighter. Asking for the first extension of her career was going to kill her.

When she finally opened the door, she did a double take. The desk in the reception room was empty, the chair overturned, and a buzz of animated conversation came at her from the staff room behind. She limped quickly down the attached hallway and peered through the door. Godmothers and godfathers, crowded in a tight circle in the middle of the room, were talking in hushed tones.

"What's going on?" The Claire who stood in the entrance was her true self. Long, golden hair tumbled down her back, and a shiny platinum band designating her level-one rank crowned her head. Her gown, deep forest green and a little old school in its cut, matched the color of her eyes exactly. Other godmothers dressed in more modern clothes, but Claire was proud of her job and wasn't afraid to show it.

"Holy Succubus, Claire." A level-two-minus waved her over. "Did you hear what Pierre did?"

"No, what happened?" A chill ran down her neck. Office gossip was severely frowned upon in the FGC—a punishable offense, even. What could Pierre have done that would have everyone breaking the rule?

"He marched into Juliette's office this morning and handed in his wand. He quit."

"What?" Claire's mouth dropped open. Holy Succubus was right. In all her centuries on the job, she had never heard of such a thing.

"No joke." The level-two-minus shook her head. "He said he was never any good as a godfather, and he might as well take his chances in the human world."

"Seriously? How will he access the magic?" Claire asked.

"He can't!" A young male apprentice shuddered.

"Apparently," the level-two-minus said in a mock whisper, "Pierre told Juliette it wouldn't really be any different; he never could get much magic out of his wand. Except now the FGC couldn't track him. He came out here and announced to all of us that the FGC has us in a chokehold and he was going to be his own man."

"Wow." Claire's mouth went dry. No one had ever left the FGC of his or her own accord. That was unbelievably stupid... and maybe the bravest thing she had ever heard.

"I don't know why we're all so surprised." A wizened old godmother put in her two cents. "I'm not sure why it hasn't happened sooner." She waved a hand at the digital clock on one bare wall. Large red numbers ticked upward to document all deadlines to the millisecond. "Look at the conditions we're working under."

"What will he do?" Claire still couldn't get her head around someone willingly giving up his wand. Carothann was a part of her. It would be like cutting off a hand.

"Maybe he's just rediscovering his roots," the level-two-minus said. "You know we're supposed to be part human."

"It's the other part he should be discovering," the old godmother said. "We don't even know what it is."

"You don't think he's going to work for the GA, do you?" the apprentice asked.

"Oh, don't be stupid." The old godmother turned to face the young man. "What would the Guardian Angels want with a godfather? They hate us."

"Think of all the intel he could give them. All they'd have to do is look in his eyes and he would be their slave," the apprentice said with certainty.

"No. It doesn't work that way." The level-two-minus pulled them back on track. "Administration was on Pierre's ass constantly. It couldn't have been much fun for him. He hadn't closed a case in a long time."

A shiver ran through Claire at the thought of Abby turning up at the party only to go home alone and possibly naked. Letting the salesman dance the night away with a woman who wasn't her client didn't sound like such a good idea in the harsh light of the FGC office and this conversation. "It's getting really hard to close a case these days."

"Oh, honey, you don't have to worry," the old godmother said. "You're fairy godmother royalty. Cinderella, Sleeping Beauty, that Middleton girl. You—"

Her last word echoed around her. Everyone had gone completely silent. Claire twisted her head and gasped.

Her boss—tall, imposing, and sexy as hell—stood at the back of the room. She wore a shimmering gown whose panels fell straight and snug, calling all sorts of attention to her tight breasts and long waist. Her auburn hair was swept into a simple bun so as not to compete with her stellar body. She would have been really something, if not for the imperious glare she threw out into the room.

"Dragon balls," the apprentice said quietly.

The level-two-minus took in a quick breath. Fear flashed in her eyes.

"Don't worry," Claire said grimly. "I'm pretty sure she's here for me." She swung toward the woman at the door. Their gazes met.

Juliette inclined her head to the windowed office in the back, and Claire carefully threaded her way through the frozen operatives to join her.

Juliette shook her head disapprovingly as they entered the office. A list of open cases, like a whiteboard in a hospital nurses' station, magically hovered against the back wall. Most of the cases glittered with golden letters. Only two names flashed in red. Pierre's and hers.

Juliette pointed to the board. "So you want to tell me about that?"

Claire stalled with a deep breath. She would have to play this one very carefully. "I made a game-time decision. He wasn't right for Abby."

"What were you thinking, Claire?" Juliette's eyes flashed. "You know protocol better than anyone. You always need to clear any deviations with us first. We just can't have godmothers going off on their own."

"Yes. I know, Juliette, but he was too easily diverted." That much was true, but a shiver of fear ran through her. What had she been thinking? "And Abby wasn't into—"

"Claire," Juliette raised her hands. "Please tell me you aren't in here to ask for an extension."

Claire swallowed and nodded as if she were a schoolgirl being called into the principal's office. "Sorry." And when Juliette didn't answer, she added, "It happens to everyone."

"Not to you. Usually, you can close this kind of case in your sleep." Juliette made a show of pressing one hand to her temple.

It was true, so Claire said nothing.

"Look. This isn't the time for a slump," Juliette said. "The FGC is under a lot of scrutiny right now. First, the Guardian Angels start stealing our clients, and now Pierre..." She sighed deeply. "We need to show results, not problems. You do know they just shut down the Santa Barbara office, right?"

Claire nodded.

"And now you're coming in here with problems you've created and making a bad day even worse."

A bad day. That was an understatement. Upper Administration had to be crawling all over Juliette. It was plain poor luck that Pierre had been under her jurisdiction. He was a terrible godfather, always had been. But Juliette was also the worst kind of middle management. Unengaged and inefficient until something went wrong, and then it was all about covering her own ass.

"Let me be clear." Juliette's voice cut into her thoughts. "You're in here not because of one silly girl who dreams of being more than a receptionist at a dog food company—"

"Paper," Claire said, not quite under her breath.

"Paper. Dog food. No matter. This is about our way of life. No one wants a fairy godmother anymore. Girls these days want to find their own path. And some of them don't even want men. And I'm not talking about the way you don't want males. Love is love. The FGC has always been up to handling that. No, I'm talking about financial independence and feminist causes. Where true soul mates don't even make an appearance."

Claire rubbed her chin. Women these days might have a point. After all, she had risen to the top of her game without a soul mate. It had worked for her.

"We need to find a way to reinvent ourselves to fit into these new values." Juliette's voice had risen a whole octave as she spoke. She caught herself and smoothed back a curl that had escaped the bun. "If we're going to survive, we need to be the force of the future, not the force of the past."

For half a second, Claire had thought about pulling a pom-pom out of the air and waving it with her every word. Juliette ate up any kind of butt-kissing, and she was right. The FGC did need to reinvent itself. The name alone needed to be more gender-fluid for starters. But for now, Claire just had to get through this meeting and figure out a better solution for Abby. Let Upper Administration figure out the big issues. Maybe, though, it was the same issue.

"Of course, Juliette," she said.

"Good. I have to know that you're all-in. That I can trust you. To do what I say, when I say it."

Now Claire flinched. What the hell was going on? This conversation was all over the place. Abby, the Guardian Angels, and now… Was Juliette really rescinding the one thing that made this job palatable? Her autonomy in the field.

Juliette stared down her nose, waiting for an answer.

Claire resisted the impulse to tell her boss where to shove it and said instead, "You can, Juliette. I'm here for the FGC." When Juliette still didn't answer, she added, "And for you too, of course."

"Excellent. I'll extend the deadline on case number 69317."
Juliette flicked her own wand, Baltine, a lovely red Manzanita
branch. Claire's name and case on the board flickered back into
gold. "But no more pussyfooting around. I'm going out on a
limb for you. Close it as soon as possible."

"Right." Claire started toward the door, carefully favoring
her hurt shin. Thankfully, this whole horrible conversation
seemed to be drawing to a close.

"Oh, and one more thing. I need to ask for your help with
another case." Juliette's voice turned sultry.

Claire groaned inwardly. Everyone knew that Juliette only
trotted out this voice when the stakes were high.

She turned back. "What case?"

"This one." The thickest folder that Claire had ever seen
appeared out of nowhere and hovered magically in the dead
space between them. Juliette gracefully plucked the file out of
the air with her long fingers and handed it to Claire.

"Read the whole thing. We can do a meet and greet with
the girl first thing in the morning, and then we'll sit down and
strategize how we'll run the case."

"We?" Surely Juliette had misspoken.

"Yes, we. This is one of those cases that will make the FGC
relevant again. I believe it came straight from the director's
office in Paris. And I thought…we could work it together."

Claire's mind spun. Administration never worked the field.
"I normally work solo."

"I know, and maybe partnering up is one of the policies we
need to look into as we reinvent the Fairy Godmother Council
for the twenty-first century."

Claire said nothing. Wrapping her mind around having
Juliette as a partner, or even just having a partner in general,
made her head spin. "Juliette. Look, I—"

"Do you want to end up like that?" Juliette pointed to the board behind her. Pierre's name flashed red once and then went black. He was no longer an FGC operative.

Claire flinched. Juliette, inept as she was, was the queen of low blows. Who would Claire be without her job?

"Okay. We can work it together."

"Perfect. Contact me first thing in the morning."

Claire limped out of the office. Her night wasn't over. Medical always took forever. A long session would give her time to think, though. How on earth was she going to work two cases at once? Especially when one of those cases involved a new *partner*?

No good deed ever went unpunished.

The next couple of days were going to be living proof.

CHAPTER 3

Two Days Earlier

THE NEXT MORNING, CLAIRE CARRIED a latte and the huge folder into the tiny private garden behind her Santa Monica bungalow. The patio held just a small wrought-iron table and chairs but was surrounded by a riot of color. Pink-purple flowers hung like delicate lanterns from several fuchsia bushes, and in one corner a red bougainvillea spread over a fanned trellis. She loved this house. It was only a couple of blocks from the bluffs, and a gentle ocean breeze almost always blew through its windows.

Like everyone else, she had balked when the FGC had withdrawn the magic-housing allotment early in the twentieth century. Before then, anything—the side of a mountain, an oak tree, a carpet of bluebell flowers—could be a luxurious home. All it took was a boatload of magic. Now they had to find housing on their own. The FGC gave them a monthly stipend of human currency—far easier to come by than magic, they were told.

Nearly a century later, the grumbling about the policy had not stopped. But once Claire had gotten over the horror of "hiding in plain sight," as Upper Administration had called it, she actually preferred the new way. No one was going to chop down this house for firewood or flooring while she was out, and since the LA lifestyle was all about moving up, no one stayed in this neighborhood long enough to discover that she wasn't aging like a human.

Juliette's file sat like a brick on her patio table. Dread curled through her. She should have stayed up late to read the tome, but the two unsatisfactory meetings with Abby and Juliette, not to mention Medical, had worn her out. The day hadn't been particularly hard, just incredibly annoying.

Do I even like my job anymore?

Pierre and a dozen questions popped into her brain. When he quit, had he thrown his wand on Juliette's desk, or had he passed it to her hand? Had he gone out with a whimper or a bang? Had his wand reached out for him as he walked out of the office?

With a deep sigh, she flipped open the folder.

Fairy Godmother Council: Official Document

FRANCESCA (Frankie) HARRIS
Case No. 69356

CASE HISTORY:
Father: Ben Harris—Hollywood producer of family sitcoms: Bundle of Joy, The Bounce House, Bring Me Home

Mother: Lori Harris (deceased)—Professor of religious philosophy, UCLA

Mother died tragically at Frankie's birth. Father threw himself into work. Produced one hit sitcom after another. Ben remarried Dione Vershon, Hollywood helicopter parent and manager, seven years later. They met when Ben was casting for the pilot of The Bounce House. *Dione auditioned her twin girls, Porsche and Perry, for the role of adorable two-year-old girl. The twins got the part, and Dione got Ben. Ben died of cancer when Frankie was twelve. Dione inherited control of the estate until Frankie comes of age at twenty-one.*

CURRENT HISTORY:
Frankie, eighteen, has recently returned to the Harris estate, now controlled by her stepmother and stepsisters. She previously ran away and for three years was nowhere to be found. Dione claims this absence illustrates that she has no real interest in the estate. Dione has hired the best probate lawyers in the country to contest the will. If they are successful, Frankie will never have a dime to her name.

OCCUPATION:
Artist.

SUGGESTED ACTION:
Locate client and find a perfect male match for her.
Happily ever after.
Attributes for ideal partner: male, kind, older, impervious to the lure of money. Rich in his own right. Client must be returned to a genteel lifestyle where she is taken care of and can indulge in her art.

That was it? She had no idea who this girl was—what made her tick or what exactly would give her the happily ever after. Why did it always have to be a relationship, anyway? Juliette had been angry when she went off about the FGC being obsolete, but Claire had actually been thinking about it for a while. The FGC needed to embrace results other than relationships as victories. That would launch them into the twenty-first century kicking and screaming. The problem was, the FCG wasn't into real change. They were comfortable with finding soul mates and birth blessings because those results were traditional and easy. Real innovation required a rabble-rouser who could walk the hard path and wasn't afraid to step on a few toes. Definitely not Juliette. There would never be any real change at the LA branch under her leadership.

Whatever. Not her call. Way above her pay grade.

Claire turned the top sheet over to make sure she hadn't missed anything of importance. Nope. Nothing. She jerked her bottom jaw from side to side, forcing the muscles around her mouth to relax. If this case was as important as Juliette said it was, she could use a little help here.

Weird. There was no stamp from a preparer or an administrator, and the layout was different than normal—more pages, but less info, somehow. She flipped through a colored graph and several pie charts and stopped at a diagram of boxes splattered with red dots. Claire turned the paper first one way and then the other. The visuals, pretty as they were, didn't make much sense. Juliette said this file had come from the head office.

They, of all people, should do a better job. They're just going through the motions too. That's what really needs to change.

She slapped the file closed. Nothing inside was going to help her. Her main problem was Juliette and whatever her true agenda was. She gulped down the last bit of latte, which had long since gone cold, and went inside to call her boss.

As soon as she entered the house, Carothann reached out for her. Tendrils of golden magic leaped out from where the wand stayed when it wasn't in her pocket: a red, velvet-lined box on her desk. Bright feelers curled into the air, searching for her. She and the wand had been connected like this right from start. The moment she had walked into the FGC wand repository as an apprentice, Carothann had nudged at her like a puppy asking for attention. Now fingers of magic wound around her arms and torso and gently tugged her to the desk.

She had been taught—all FGC operatives had—that the godmother's intentions gave power to a wand, and practice made them both stronger. But from the moment Claire had clutched Carothann in her hand, she'd suspected the wand was more than it was letting on. What was holding it back, she had no idea. But there was power in its heartwood. The tip blinked, revealing just one of its many abilities. Juliette had left a message.

She directed a thought to the wand, and Juliette's voice filled the air.

"Claire. Something's come up. Why don't you head over to the client, do a little meet and greet, and then you can catch me up to speed."

Claire rolled her eyes. *Figures.* Juliette was going to let her do the heavy lifting and then swoop in at the last minute to take all the credit. She sighed and stilled her mind as she zeroed in on the fact that this case was not about her or Juliette; it was about a girl—hopefully, for once, a deserving one—who needed help.

"Take me to Frankie," Claire said. Carothann pulsated in her hand, and they both slipped into the golden stream of magic that filled the room.

The smell of urine and neglect hit Claire before she had fully materialized in the narrow downtown alley. Old, deteriorating buildings rose on either side, and the homeless slept fitfully on the ground in clumps. Trash, and God knew what else, lay in thick piles between them. Still, it wasn't the worst place she'd ever run a case.

She flicked Carothann. Magic swirled through her body like a tumbling rush of endorphins and ran up her spine. Blood surged; muscles contracted and released, and bones folded inward. The tingling started in her toes and raced everywhere. The pleasure verged on euphoria but ebbed before it could take hold. Transformations—one of the perks of the job—never got old.

Claire shook her new body. For this morning's case, she had chosen an anime character that decorated a billboard outside her favorite udon place. She sported a small mouth, a dainty nose, and big, round eyes. Dark hair floated around her head almost as a separate organism. Frankie was an artist, so she should respond to this look. Speaking of Frankie…where was she?

A flash of movement from the dead end of the alley caught her gaze. A figure shrouded in a black hoodie darted back and forth in front of the bricks. Each hand held a can of spray paint, and the pressurized pssst of her work echoed in the small space. She moved fast; elaborate, interlocking letters in blue and gold quickly took shape on the wall. The style was so wild; Claire couldn't make heads or tails of it.

Artist, her ass. Frankie was a tagger. A bomber. Nothing but a common criminal.

She let out a deep sigh and put one foot forward as she began the long march down the alley. The muscles in her shoulders tensed. It was going to be yet another hard case. But all she had to do was make contact and then report back to Juliette. If she wanted in on this case, let her make the next move. Let her see for herself how hard operating in the field was when the girls were—

Get out!

The thought exploded into her mind in white-hot shards. Its sudden appearance chased out all reason. The desire to run away surged through her whole body, compelling her to move. She had spun on her heel before she fought off the impulse to sprint back to where she had come from.

Mind control!

Son of a banshee. A guardian angel was here. Mind control and how to resist it were key subjects in the FGC workshops, but no facilitator had mentioned the violence of the invasion.

She scanned the alley left and right. Nothing. But that didn't mean a GA operative wasn't there. Learning about their incredible ability to glamour—to resonate at a higher frequency and vanish—had taken up a whole afternoon of professional development.

"Frankie's mine!" she hissed through clenched teeth and raised Carothann before her like a weapon.

GET OUT!

Pain shot through her head as an impulse to flee, even stronger now, tugged at her body.

"Fat chance! This is my client. Tell the GA I'm not backing down."

She forced her feet to move down the alley toward Frankie, who, oblivious to the nearly silent screaming match, was still throwing paint up on the wall.

NO. A piercing wail like a wraith's vibrated in her head, and Claire turned just in time to see the shimmer of the guardian angel racing full tilt down the alley toward her.

It was all motion and power. She couldn't make out any features—the glamour was still strong around it. But she could tell that it was coming right at her.

Claire's heartbeat thrashed in her ears, and her breath came out in rasps. Information from the FGC handbook popped into her head. She flicked Carothann, and a golden flash, supposedly as deadly as a spree of bullets, flew straight at the angel.

And bounced harmlessly off it.

The angel ate up the space between them as if it were inches instead of yards.

Claire backed away with quick, jerky steps. Forget going on the offense. She flicked Carothann again. Magic threads wove into a shimmering mesh, instantly settling over her as she switched tactics to a defensive stance. Energy hummed through the air. Would the shield be any protection against the force of nature barreling down on her?

Claire screwed her eyes shut, braced her feet firmly against the mesh, and waited for impact.

And waited…and waited.

Claire's eyes popped open; the angel was already three strides beyond her, racing to the back of the alley, a flaming sword outstretched in one hand.

Claire's legs almost buckled. The angel wasn't after her; it was after Frankie! Was it going to kill her?

"Stop!" Claire cried.

Frankie spun at the cry and took in Claire with one glance. Her body stiffened. "I'm not doing anything." She tucked the cans behind her back and met Claire's gaze with a teenager's practiced innocence. Clearly, she couldn't see the angel rushing right at her. Or the burning sword swinging right for her head.

"Duck!" Claire's warning echoed through the alley.

Frankie crouched at the last possible second, but the sword had already struck to the right of her and was lodged in something dark and scaly that had impossibly skittered up from the pavement.

Was that a freaking...demon?

Growling, the monster threw out a dark, claw-like hand toward the angel's head.

The angel dodged the blow a second before the talons could hit. It bounced up and stabbed at the monster, so fast that the sword blurred through the air, a dart of light and heat.

The creature was just as quick. It twisted from the thrust, taking the blow on its massive, scaly arm, and swiveled to give the angel its back, layered with thick black scales. Shifting its attention to Frankie, it unhinged its jaw. Two razor-sharp rows of teeth shone in the morning light. The creature lunged at the girl with another inhuman growl. Frankie couldn't actually see the danger—it must have been shielded and glamoured as well—but she could certainly feel it.

"Oh my God!" she cried. The cans clattered to the ground, and she flattened herself against the wall in an attempt to get away from the creature. The monster took the angel's next blow harmlessly on its armored back and lurched, mouth wide open, toward the girl.

Help me! The angel's scream burst in Claire's head.

This time, Claire let the suggestion take hold of her and shake her out of her lethargy. She jumped to the angel's side.

The monster had turned and was waiting for Claire's arrival. Its talons clutched around her throat as soon as her feet hit her mark. Claire's breath hissed out of her as the creature squeezed and crushed her windpipe. She crumbled. Darkness without end poured into her, running through the talons and down her neck, boring its way to her soul. Dizziness and pain hit her as if she had been pierced with a thousand knives. Her vision went black, and her world began to narrow.

The whoosh of a rippling flame slashed through the air. Metal clashed against bones, and an intense heat scorched her cheek. A shriek that wasn't human filled the air as the hand around her throat loosened. The darkness receded like a tsunami wave. She gasped as the air flooded back into her lungs and sight returned to her eyes.

The monster pulled its injured arm to its chest and turned its rage back on Frankie. It clamped its good hand around her shoulder and began to drag her down into the gaping hole in the pavement that hadn't been there a moment ago.

Frankie cried out. Her hands slashed at thin air as she twisted and turned.

Together. Now.

The angel's thoughts exploded in her mind, but this time without pain. The blinding light, instead, gave her strength, and she spun Carothann to the monster, certain of what she had to do next.

The angel was already poised, its sword aimed at the middle of the creature's back around heart level.

Into the sword. Claire threw the thought at her wand. Carothann bucked and surged, like a horse released from the bridle. Magic poured from the wand and drove straight to its target. The flame on the sword turned a deep blue as godmother and angel magic coalesced. Claire poured everything she had into her wand, and Carothann jumped and twisted, red-hot, in her hand. The angel's sword vibrated as a primal humming echoed through the alley. But still, the angel didn't move.

"Come on," Claire cried. "I can't hold this much longer."

Just as the monster was about to sink into the ground with Frankie, the angel lunged and slid its sword into the monster's back. It plunged through the thick hide as if it were fine leather. The creature dropped Frankie away from the hole, shrieking in agony.

The angel gripped the sword with both hands and dug in deeper. The blade popped right through the front of the creature with a shuddering crack.

The monster's eyes blazed with fury and then went cold. The life ran out of it, and it, too, crumpled, dropping out of existence as it tumbled back into the hole.

The smell of burning, rotted flesh rolled over Claire. Gagging, she almost fell to her knees as well, but the angel pulled her back up with one hand and collected Frankie with the other. The girl was limp in the angel's grasp.

When had Frankie fainted? Claire hoped it had been sooner rather than later for the girl's sake.

The angel pulled both of them down the alley and deposited Frankie gently on the ground next to a homeless man who still, after everything, snored softly. Was this the angel's doing? If so, the angel's magic was strong—stronger than hers.

"You okay?" it asked.

As she turned to face her rescuer, Claire's eyes widened. Its voice out loud was nothing like the battle cry in her head. The intonation was soft and melodious and circled around her, soothing her shattered nerves like a balm.

Claire nodded, unable to speak, and raised a hand to her cheek—not burned at all.

"Good." The flame on the sword died, and the creature sheathed it in a scabbard on its back. She hadn't noticed that before.

In fact, there were lots of things to observe now that it had dropped completely into her dimension. She took the chance and ran her gaze up the angel's body. It was tall, slender, and taut with muscle. Some sort of silver clothing clung to it, moving as if it were more liquid than material. Holy Harpy, what a great figure.

Actually, now that Claire was looking carefully, the creature read female. Narrow, boyish hips, but there was something definitely female about the way she stood and the swelling at her chest. That Claire had ever thought of her as an *it* was criminal. In fact—a shiver ran down her spine—the angel was drop-dead gorgeous, all lightness and grace.

No wings. That was a surprise. She had always assumed that angels had wings like the mythologies said. Not that the folklore got anything right about fairy godmothers. As far as anyone knew, there was no fairy in them at all.

The angel bent down to draw Frankie's arm into a more comfortable position, and her shirt, flowing around her, caught the early morning sun and glistened as if she stood under a silver waterfall. That wasn't in the mythologies either.

Claire's gaze traveled to her face. Her jaw was strong, her cheekbones chiseled. Her dark, straight hair was cropped short at the sides and long on top. Dark bangs fell over her eyes. Claire's breath caught in her throat.

Wow. How had she not noticed the eyes sooner?

They had no color. Live flame danced where the irises should be: bottomless pools of light and heat. Try as she might, she couldn't pull her gaze away. She was falling into their orbits. One more moment and she would be gone.

Claire blinked repeatedly and jerked her head away. Enough of this. No wonder humans fell under their glamour.

Never let a client look an angel in its eyes. Once they've imprinted, there is no way to break the spell. Even an apprentice knew that. She couldn't let those eyes anywhere near Frankie. If she had a hard time dragging herself away, Frankie would be lost. Claire shifted toward the front of the alley so the angel would have to face away from her client.

Be polite, don't engage, get her out of my case. That was now the plan.

"Thank you for saving me from that...that..." She looked back to empty space in front of the brick wall at the end of the alley. Only the pulpy arm remained, and already it was melting into nothingness.

"Demon," the angel said. "For lack of a better word."

A new rush of adrenaline surged through Claire. A true, honest-to-goodness demon. Was there really a plan for this scenario?

"I'll take the thanks," the angel said, "but I didn't save you. We defeated it together." She ran her gaze down Claire's body. "Actually, I think we made a good team."

Claire's stomach churned. "The Guardian Angels and the Fairy Godmother Council can't team up. I—"

"You know, that's only a rule on your side. But don't worry. I'm not here for Frankie. She's all yours." To punctuate her point, the angel reached up and touched Claire briefly on her forearm. As soon as her fingers dropped, a lightness surrounded Claire, and the last vestiges of the demon's darkness in her chest curled up into thin wisps and withered away. Her fingers, her touch, were the softest Claire had ever felt.

"Why...why are you here?" Claire forced her mind to focus.

The angel gave her a look that she couldn't read. "The demon. Why else?" She smiled softly. "Stay safe, fairy godmother."

The angel disappeared into the morning air with a soft poof. No glitter, no golden light, just a slight breeze that ruffled down the alley and brought with it a whiff of freshly cut pine and mountain lavender. The homeless all around Claire sighed as the scent of the forest drifted into their dreams.

Something made her look back down the alley to the blue and gold swirlings of Frankie's graffiti. From this far back, letters and then a word took shape and rose like a beacon to whoever passed this way. The letters curled in on themselves and formed the word *HOPE*.

Frankie.

Between the angel's eyes and her touch, Claire had almost forgotten. She dropped to her knees and studied the poor girl on the ground. Honey-brown hair framed a classically beautiful face—high cheekbones and full lips. Her features were about as symmetrical as it got. Take away the hoodie and the grime, and she could be a true princess on looks alone. The story of her mother's death and interfering stepmother was almost archetypal. And—Claire glanced back down the alley at the masterpiece on the wall—she was, after all, supremely talented.

Was this deserving girl the case she had been waiting for all these years?

Claire gently shook her shoulder. She wanted to be the first thing Frankie saw when she awoke. She didn't think the angel was coming back, but who knew with their type. Every FGC lecture told her that she didn't want to be the fool who let her guard down.

Frankie's eyes blinked open. They widened, and her breath quickened before she registered Claire. "Oh my God. Where is it?" She scuttled back against the alley wall and shook her head violently.

Claire reached out an arm to comfort the girl, but Frankie batted it away, and so Claire just pointed down the alley to the remains of the demon. "Don't worry. It's gone."

They stared at the remnants of the arm that were oozing into the cracks in the pavement.

"That…that was what was attacking me?" Frankie asked, her eyes going completely round.

Claire nodded.

"I couldn't see it. It was all around me, but I couldn't see it."

Frankie's gaze darted around the alley, obviously searching for answers. None existed.

Claire's heart went out to her. For the first time, maybe ever, she knew exactly how confusing a brush with magic could feel.

"It's over now. It's gone," she said, unsure whether she was trying to convince herself or Frankie.

"What was it?"

"I don't know. But whatever it was, it's not going to hurt you anymore."

Frankie's brows furrowed. "You did that? You killed it?"

"In part," Claire wasn't going to lie to the girl, but the whole truth wouldn't do either of them any good.

"How?"

Claire met her scrutiny. Frankie's breath had softened, and she was staring back at Claire with clear, curious eyes.

"I'm your fairy godmother," Claire jumped right in, tilting her head back and waiting for disbelief to take root in the girl's gaze.

Instead, Frankie threw herself into Claire's arms, nearly sending them both toppling over into someone's treasure trove of aluminum cans. "Woo-hoo! I knew you would come. I just knew it."

Claire pulled them both to their feet as a true smile spread across her face. She couldn't remember the last time an introduction had been this easy.

"Ever since the first dream, I prayed that someone would come and help me." Frankie's voice trembled. "I thought it would be my mother somehow. She's dead, you know."

Claire nodded.

"I thought she would find a way to come back. And when she didn't, I thought maybe someone like you... I mean, I've always kind of believed in magic...and now, when I need you the most, here you are."

"Yes, here I am," Claire said, and the knot that had taken up residence in her stomach since Abby loosened.

"And you really are a fairy godmother? Like, with a wand and wings and wishes that come true?"

"I am. Well, no wings." Claire swung around to show Frankie her empty back. Wings must be a universal misconception. "But yes to a wand that grants wishes." She pulled Carothann out of her sleeve with a shower of golden sparks and trumpet fanfare.

"Cool," Frankie said, sounding like such a teenager that Claire laughed. "Can I see?" And before her motion registered, Frankie had grabbed Carothann and was pulling it out of Claire's hand. The wand writhed in protest.

"Don't!" Claire cried and held tight. She tugged from her end while Frankie yanked from hers. A soft crack echoed off the alley's brick walls.

Magic, sharp and ragged, surged through the wand. It bucked away from Frankie's touch, and Claire pulled it back forcibly as her heartbeat raced and adrenaline spiked in her veins.

"Sorry," Frankie said quickly.

Claire studied the wand, turning it over and over in her hands. It looked okay; it felt okay. The crack must just be Carothann's alarm at being touched by a stranger.

Frankie must have seen her worried expression, for her face fell and her bottom lip began to tremble.

"Don't worry, sweetheart. I think it's fine." Claire gave the wand a half flick, and the newspaper covering a man to her side smoothed out into a thick blanket. Claire let out the breath that had hitched in her throat.

"See?" Claire dropped her shoulders and forced herself to relax. "It's just that wands are linked to their godmothers. They don't like to be handled by anyone else. They can't deal with it."

"I am so sorry." Frankie rubbed a hand across her eyes. "All I want to do is fall asleep at night and not have the dreams. I thought this would help."

"Your dreams?" She slipped Carothann back into the pocket of magic. "What happens in your dreams?"

"They're full of darkness." Frankie stiffened. "Could that thing—whatever it was—come at me in my dreams?"

"I don't know." Claire bit her lip and wished she had asked the angel a few questions rather than rushing her off to protect her turf.

"It doesn't matter," Frankie said. "You're here now. You won't let anything bad happen to me, right?"

"Right." Her heart raced. All this was way out of her league. For the first time in her career, she needed help.

Harpies and hags. Maybe she needed management after all. Who would have thought?

Claire stepped calmly into Juliette's office at branch headquarters. The horror of what had happened in the alley was behind her now, and she was trying to figure out how to play this meeting. Demons, to say the least, were the kind of anomaly that got cases booted upstairs to Upper Administration. And since Juliette had not been there, she could spin whatever had gone wrong as Claire's fault.

"Juliette. I need to tell you—"

Juliette held up two signs. "One or two?"

"Something happened this morning—"

"No. Don't think about it. Just give me your gut reaction."

Juliette jostled the signs in the air, waiting for an answer.

Was this what had prevented her from attending the morning's meeting? Tension flooded into Claire's shoulders as she stared at the signs in Juliette's outstretched hands. One was abstract black lines that gave the impression of a wand with a star at its top. Two, on the other hand, was a green, cartoonish burst, like a firework blast with trailing sparklers.

"We need a logo and a brand. I'm trying to extract who the FGC really is. This one is bold, modern." She flapped the more abstract drawing in the air. "Black says we're sophisticated. That the FGC has gravitas." She placed it on her desk and held out the firework burst. "But this one is a little more whimsical, and green announces to the world that we are caring and fresh—that we'll put your needs ahead of ours. With today's emphasis on—"

"Juliette." Claire grabbed number two and placed it on the desk as well. "I need to talk to you about what happened at the meet and greet with our client today."

"What?" she asked offhandedly, her attention still shifting between the two signs.

"Well, for starters the GA was there."

Juliette's head jerked up. "Did they—?"

"No, she wasn't there for Frankie, or so she said. But get this. The angel was after a...demon."

Juliette sat back in her chair, her body tensing. "A demon?"

"That's what the angel called it."

"Imagine that," Juliette said as if she really couldn't.

"Whatever it was, it looked like it was after Frankie. In fact, she told me it had been in her dreams. Juliette, what on earth is going on here? What kind of case is this?"

Juliette's eyes narrowed, and it occurred to Claire with a sudden intuition that Juliette didn't have any idea either.

"Who did you say this case came from?" Claire asked. "There wasn't a preparer's stamp on it."

"From the top. I'll shoot a message upstairs to find out who specifically."

Why didn't you ask when it came in? That would've been my first question.

"That would be really helpful," Claire said instead.

Juliette shuffled both logos to the side of her desk. "Anything else I should know?"

Claire glanced down at her bare arm. The spot where the angel had touched her was still tingling.

"No."

To be fair, she had stepped into the office with the intention of telling Juliette everything, especially about her and the angel teaming up. But now, when the question was dangled in her face, she shook her head. If the truth came out later, she could just say she thought it was implied. She didn't know how

Juliette would react to such a confession, and if she were being honest, she wanted to keep the angel to herself for just a little longer. *Stupid, right?*

Juliette rubbed her chin and scowled. "How is Carothann holding up after the demon fight? Did it imprint on Frankie? You didn't leave her unmonitored or unprotected, did you?"

"No. Of course not. There was a little mishap in the alley, but it doesn't seem to be any worse for wear. Carothann and Frankie are bonded. I set up a protective barrier as well before I sent her home." Claire knew Juliette was just covering her own ass now, but she was almost insulted. How dare she imply Claire had not taken every precaution to protect their client. "Alarms will ring if anything goes wrong. We'll be the first to know."

"What kind of little mishap? Can I see your wand?" She held out her hand.

"What?" Claire bristled. Now she definitely was insulted. Juliette had crossed a line, several in fact. Was Juliette, who never went into the field anymore, questioning Claire's ability? Her! A level-one-plus operative whose record, until the last two days, had been spotless.

But she couldn't refuse. If she did, a demerit would magically appear by her name, now floating in two lines on the case board behind Juliette. So Claire pulled Carothann from the magic pocket at her side. It slid into her hand as if it had been made for her grip, and she held it up for Juliette's inspection. Why was everyone so focused on Carothann today? Surely, she wasn't going to touch it. Wands could easily be infected by anyone's intention.

Juliette let her hand drop, maybe realizing she had overstepped. Instead, she made a circle with two fingers.

Claire twisted the wand until the two bands that shone from within at the bottom were facing Juliette. One, bright green, for Abby. The other, maroon, for Frankie.

"Maroon. That's interesting."

It was. The wand chose the color of the light circle when it connected with a client. Maroon was unusual, especially since it was edged with black. What the hell did that mean? She had no idea, so she said, "I think Carothann just knows how important this case is."

"Why don't you take it to Wand Tech when you get a chance. Just to make sure it is fine." Juliette wouldn't meet her gaze. "I'll talk to Upper Administration and get back to you," she said lightly. "Please wait until I do, and then we'll go to Frankie together."

Claire was just about to tuck Carothann away when the green band, the one belonging to Abby, started blinking and a soft but high-pitched alarm filled the room. Abby's case was in trouble.

"Frankie?" Juliette asked.

"No. Abby."

"Go to her," Juliette said. "Get this case closed so we can concentrate on the important one. Don't fail me again."

Again? When had she failed Juliette before? No time to voice that thought. She closed her fist around the wand, and with barely a thought, it pushed her into the magic stream and to Abby. God only knew what trouble she was in now.

Fully invisible, Claire popped up in a self-serve yogurt store in the middle of Hollywood. Pop music blared over the speakers, and lime-green and magenta stripes swooped around the stainless-steel machines embedded in the back wall.

Abby stood by the Berry Blast flavor at the far end, laughing and cooing as she tried to pull down the knob of the yogurt machine.

"It's not coming out." Her voice sounded girlish and silly.

By her side stood a very handsome man with spiky hair and tats running down both arms. One hand rested on Abby's hip while he slid the other over her hand on the machine. Bright blue yogurt poured into her cup.

"Oh, I wasn't pulling hard enough."

"You can never pull too hard, baby. I like it rough."

Abby laughed.

Claire cringed. How could Abby be so stupid? You didn't need magic to see how wrong this man was. Claire didn't like to stereotype, though, so just for kicks, she looked past the baggy pants, the black ball cap, and the red bandana just peeking out of his back pocket. This man was trouble to his core.

Even so, Claire had to bite back a smile. She was back in her element. No demons, no GA, just an easy push to get Abby back on track.

She zipped down the empty hallway to the back of the store and flicked Carothann. Magic like lightning ran up her backbone. Heat and light radiated out to all points of her body. A six-year-old girl, complete with a missing front tooth and long braids, appeared next to the women's bathroom. Tears flooded the little girl's eyes, and when she rounded the corner into the store, the child Claire was sobbing freely.

"Mommy, Mommy." Claire had a kid's hysterics down perfectly. She approached the pair. "Where did you go?"

Abby swung wildly around, looking for the child's mother.

Claire reached out to her and tugged on her black yoga pants at the hip, the exact place where the man's hand lay. He jerked back as if he'd been stung.

"Mommy, Mommy. I waited in the bathroom just like you told me to, but you never came back."

Shock mixed with disgust spread over the man's face. "You got a kid?"

"No. I don't. This is not—"

"Forget this shit." He stuffed his full yogurt cup into a bin of cookie pieces and stomped off.

"Wait!" Abby cried, but the man didn't hesitate. She glared down at Claire, whose eyes had instantly dried up. "What the fuck?"

"Not your Prince Charming," Claire said in her normal voice and shrugged her six-year-old shoulders.

Abby's eyes narrowed as she stared at the child Claire for a long moment. "You!"

The young man at the cash register snapped a large textbook shut. "You both okay over there? Little girl, is everything okay?"

Claire pulled Abby's hand down into hers. "Yeah, my mommy just got confused. That happens sometimes."

The young man cocked his head. "You know, I could get someone if you wanted…"

"No. We're good." Abby dumped her yogurt and marched Claire out of the store.

"Hey, you've got to pay for those, you know. Once they're in the cups, they're—"

The revving engine of a tricked-out car drowned out the man's voice as a restored GTO sped away. Abby frowned. "Oh my God. Is that his car?" She yanked Claire around to face her. "He was going to ask me out. I could be riding in that car right now!"

"He wasn't for you. Believe me. You couldn't do worse."

Abby tugged again at Claire's arm. "Look—"

"You better be nice to me. The man inside already thinks you're a thief and maybe even something worse. Watch out. He's reaching for his phone." Claire flicked her wand, and a ten-dollar bill appeared near the man's hand. His brow creased as he looked from the money to Claire and Abby outside the store.

Claire smiled and threw her arms around Abby in a great bear hug. "You better hug me back."

Abby did but gnashed her teeth.

The man inside dropped his cell back onto the counter and slid the money into the cash register.

"Come on, Mom. Let's get out of here." Claire pulled Abby down the sidewalk and out of the young man's sight.

"I can't believe anyone at all would buy you as my kid. My kid would be a lot cuter than—"

"Abby," Claire said. "I can't help you if you can't help yourself."

"What the hell does that mean?"

Irritation rose in Claire, but she reveled in it. She knew how to play this game. "It means show up to parties when I tell you to and don't go throwing yourself at someone who has no goodness in him at all. He would've destroyed your life."

"How could you possibly know that? He was cute."

"Do we have to go over this again? I'm your fairy godmother."

Abby rolled her eyes. "Some fairy godmother. I had to walk home from that party—alone and in a borrowed coat."

"I told you what would happen. Weren't you listening? Look, you've got to get on board here."

Abby snorted. "On board with what? You ruining my life?"

"This will go much better if you understand how all this works. We might actually find your Prince Charming. If I give you the story of Cinderella, will you at least skim it?"

"I've seen the movie. I don't want any mice, fat or thin. They were total nutjobs."

"Try again. With the version I'll give you. No mice. No songs."

"Fine. If I do, will you stop stalking me?"

"Really read it, and I think you'll beg me to stalk you." Claire flicked her wand, and a few blocks away an annotated edition of Cinderella dropped onto Abby's coffee table. "It's waiting for you at home."

"Fine." Abby snorted. "And a new cell phone better be waiting for me too at home. Mine stopped working with all that hocus-pocus last night."

"Fat chance."

"The new iPhone. The big one!" Abby stomped down the street, and the pop song that had been playing in the yogurt store leaped to her lips. Clearly, she was belting out the words so she could drown out any response Claire might have, but actually…she was surprisingly good. Far better than the thin voice on the radio.

Claire listened until she disappeared around the corner, and then despite knowing much better, she flicked her wand again. A shiny new iPhone, complete with an unlimited data plan, popped into existence next to the book.

She shook her head. That little flick represented three new forms to fill out since, unlike the makeovers, it was meant to last, but after this morning, who was she to deny Abby a little happiness? A demon might be right around the corner for her as well.

"That was really nice." Something shimmered by her side, and a gentle breeze smelling of a mountain forest circled around her. "I hope she appreciates the extra effort."

Claire turned to the voice, and her breath quickened.

The angel, impossibly lovely, towered over her. Her black hair ruffled in the breeze she had just created, and a slight smile played at her lips. She met Claire's gaze head-on with those crazy, flaming eyes.

"What are you doing here?" Claire's gaze darted around. "Is there another demon?"

"No." *Everything's fine, Claire.*

The last bit popped into her head like a ray of sunshine, and her heart slowed.

Claire blinked hard and tore herself away from the dancing flames. The way the angel said her name was almost like a melody. "You have me at a disadvantage. I don't know your name."

The angel laughed, and music once again filled the air. "That's right. Normally, I hang out in the shadows. Influencing people by sending a thought here or there. You know, *Step back onto the curb; a bus is coming.* That kind of thing. I never actually meet my clients, so there's no need to introduce myself."

Claire waited.

"Oh, sorry. Tamiel. Tam for short. Although I can't remember the last time anyone called me that. You can, though."

She was a chatty thing. Before today, Claire would have put hard money on angels being reserved and dignified, but this woman acted like she was starved for conversation. Claire wasn't sure she minded, though. Tamiel's voice was deep and rich with just a hint of breathiness at the edges. She had also assumed angels would sound like trumpets or choirs. Crazy. A lot of her presumptions were turning out to be wrong.

"Tamiel," she repeated. The name was strangely familiar on her tongue, as if she had said it a million times already. "Twice in one day. Is this going to turn into a habit?"

What am I doing? Am I flirting with her?

"Goodness, I hope not."

Claire winced. Not the answer she had been hoping for. Son of a banshee. She did want to flirt with Tamiel.

"I mean, I hope the reason I'm here doesn't continue." Tamiel's body stiffened slightly. "Can we talk?"

Claire nodded. She glanced around and, seeing no one, quickly morphed into her true form. The action broke about a dozen rules, but she wanted Tamiel to interact with who she really was, not some kid in pigtails.

"I know the FGC has a history of not trusting the GA. And at another point, I would love to get to the bottom of that. But you've got to believe me when I say, again, that comes from you. The FGC, not you personally, I hope..."

Claire said nothing. Every written and unwritten rule of her world told her to walk away. This could be a trap. The angels were a wily bunch.

But what if everything she had been told was wrong?

She raised her head and met Tamiel's gaze. The burning flames were soft, like a warm fire at the end of a cold day. Claire fought the desire to fall into those eyes. The desire to be bathed in that warmth was almost all-consuming.

"We at the GA feel like we're on the same side..." Tamiel raised her eyebrows as though she was challenging Claire.

"Well, the FGC kind of feels like we're playing catch-up." Claire dropped her gaze.

"You're not. You have all sorts of misconceptions about us."

"Okay," Claire said, not knowing exactly to what she was agreeing.

"Great, so that's settled."

Not quite, but Claire kept her mouth shut. Let the angel spill whatever information she'd come to share.

"That demon in the alley wasn't completely sentient, but it's programmed with a mission that obviously it will die for."

47

"To kill Frankie?"

"Or to take her somewhere. I'm not sure. Basically, I need to talk to Frankie. To see if she knows why she might be targeted. But I knew you wouldn't like that. So I came here first. We can go together."

Claire didn't know what to react to: the fact that demons were apparently around every corner, that Frankie's attack wasn't random, or that she now had two partners on this case.

"I usually work alone in the field." Although strangely, this partner seemed far better than her boss.

"This case is different," Tamiel said. "I'm sure you've already realized that."

That tactic hadn't worked with Juliette either. "I'm beginning to. More and more." Claire swiped a hand through her hair. "What do you want to talk to Frankie about?"

"Whether she has any idea why the demons would be after her."

"Demons? As in plural?"

"Oh yeah. They always come in threes. And they get stronger with each incarnation."

"Maybe you should have led with that?" Claire pulled out her wand. Frankie's ring was still maroon; no alarm was sounding. The girl, as far as Carothann was concerned, wasn't in any danger.

"And then there's this. They're always tagged by the sender. If I can just look in its eyes, we can find out who has it in for your client." Tamiel swiveled on one heel. "Meet you there?"

"Wait." Claire raised a hand. "How do I know this isn't some ploy to get my guard down and then steal Frankie from me once we get there?"

"Because it isn't."

"And I'm just supposed to accept that?"

Tamiel nodded. "I don't lie, and I told you the GA isn't in competition with the FGC."

Claire tilted her head and raised her eyebrows.

"Fine." Tamiel pulled a pair of smoking-hot sunglasses out of thin air and slid them on. They were so dark, they masked all hint of the flames in her eyes. She couldn't steal Frankie if her eyes were covered. "Better?"

"Yes." Claire flicked Carothann and slipped into the magic, wondering the whole time why her heart was racing.

As the Hollywood street faded away, she prayed that breaking the cardinal rules of the FGC was the cause, or maybe it was racing off to meet demons in another epic fight...

It couldn't be that Tamiel looked awfully sexy in those black glasses.

Could it?

Claire glanced around Frankie's room in surprise. She had expected a typical teenager's room. This was basically a laundry area with a single bed in the corner. The space was dominated by a huge washer and dryer with so many buttons and digital readouts that they might blast off to Mars at any moment. A large sink, an enormous pile of clothes, and shelves overflowing with every single detergent, dryer sheet, and stain remover known to man crowded the rest of the room. One glance reminded Claire what Frankie's job was in this household. No wonder she had run away for three years.

Frankie sat on her bed, her back to the wall, softly crying.

"What's wrong, sweetheart?" Claire rushed over to the girl. At least she was still alive and alone.

"Fairy Godmother? Is that you?" Frankie's chest heaved as she flattened herself deeper into the corner.

Claire mentally kicked herself. With all the distractions, she had forgotten about the anime version and had appeared as her real self—a stranger to Frankie.

"Yes, it's me." She opened her arms, and Frankie leaped into them. "What's wrong?"

"I'm so scared. Please don't leave me alone again. Are they coming back?"

Claire glanced at Tamiel, who stood silent and mostly glamoured in the middle of the room.

"Yes, and we need to be ready," Tamiel said, literally stepping into view as she dropped into their frequency.

"Who is she?" Frankie shrank deeper into Claire's arms.

Good question. Claire rolled a bunch of answers around in her mind and finally settled on, "A friend."

Tamiel tipped her head to Claire and smiled at Frankie. "Do you have any idea why they're after you?"

"Of course not." Her voice cracked. "I'm just hanging around, throwing down my art, and then there's this demon after me."

"Actually, demons."

Claire threw Tamiel a stern look. Good thing she didn't fraternize with her clients; she had a terrible bedside manner.

"Oh God." Frankie had taken only a second to process *demons* and now pressed into Claire. "Don't leave me," she whimpered.

"We won't, and next time we can be ready," Claire said, giving the girl a quick hug.

As if on cue, Carothann's alarm blared. The floor shook. A crack, several inches wide, sliced across the room, ending right at Frankie's feet. Roaring flames shot out of the breach. *Mother Chimera*. The next time was already here, and they were most definitely not ready.

Claire pushed Frankie behind her and jumped to Tamiel's side. The angel's blazing sword swung out in a wide arc, waiting for whatever would slither out of the fissure. Claire drew Carothann, but it looked small and weak next to the angel's glowing weapon.

From the crack, a long, sharp talon attached to a massive hand reached for the ledge, and a demon, thickly muscled and covered in the same leathery hide as the last one, pulled itself up. Even before it had cleared the breach, Tamiel's sword came down hard against its neck and hacked with repeating blows until the creature's head popped from its body.

Another demon, larger, bursting with muscle, came right behind the first one. It let out a primal wail, picked up its fallen comrade as a shield, and continued climbing.

Claire lifted Carothann. She had thought about what to do on the way over, but hadn't expected to be tested this soon. When she flicked her wand, deadly pulses of magic exploded from Carothann and whistled around the demon shield like auto-targeting missiles. They hit the second monster straight on but did no damage except to fill the air with a putrid stench.

Somewhere behind her, Frankie screamed, and Tamiel yanked Claire back as the demon lumbered out of the ground.

It heaved the dead demon up and over its shoulders and flung it toward the threesome. Tamiel vaulted in front of Claire and Frankie, waving her sword in a downward arc. A wall of flame streamed down from the weapon, and when the body hit, it exploded like a bomb. Seared demon flesh splattered every corner of the room. The curtain of flame offered some protection, but chunks landed on Claire's bare arm and ate into her flesh like acid. She wailed. Her vision tunneled. The room began to close in on her as the pain jumped from nerve to nerve. She shook the demon chunks off. Oozing, bloody welts covered her entire forearm. Fighting to stay in control, she bit her lip to tamp down the searing pain.

The demon howled. The sound vibrated with power, its evil resonating throughout the room.

Frankie whimpered, and Claire reached behind with her good arm to give the girl a quick squeeze of comfort, but her gaze remained on Tamiel.

"Tell me what to do," she said through clenched teeth. She was ready to fight, but the angel needed to send her instructions. She emptied her mind and waited.

Instead, Tamiel stepped out from behind the wall of flame, slid the sunglasses off her face, and leveled her gaze at the creature as though she was studying it.

"Yakum." Tamiel's voice cracked.

What or who would make Tamiel tremble? The thought of grabbing Frankie and fleeing to the safety of the FGC office flitted through Claire's mind. But she dumped the idea almost as soon as it came to her. Tamiel had battled twice now to save them. She couldn't abandon her.

The demon roared.

Tamiel took a running start and, leading with her sword, leaped, fast and sure. It sprang into the air to meet her head-on.

The metal of her sword clashed against the demon's outstretched talons, the force of the blow sending them both spiraling to the ground. Tamiel's sword flew out of her hand and skittered across the floor to a far corner with a clatter. She stretched out a hand for it; the sword trembled in response and began a slow slide toward her.

Sword! The word burst into Claire's mind with a bright light. Almost without thought, she flicked Carothann, and the sword raced into Tamiel's grasp.

Tamiel was on the demon in an instant—hacking and cutting.

The smell of seared flesh almost made Claire retch, but the beast seemed unaffected as it blasted Tamiel with blow after blow.

"Kill it!" Tamiel's voice was strong, but the last hit of the monster's massive fist almost had the angel on her knees. Claire didn't know how much longer she could hang on.

"Tell me what to do," she shouted over the chaos.

The answer didn't come from Tamiel. Instead, Carothann twisted in her hand, and without knowing who or what she was obeying, she leveled the wand at the creature.

She sent the thought *destroy the beast* to the wand and waited for the torrent of magic to blast out. But instead, Carothann pushed back against *her*. Little strands of magic pulsed into her palm, and like horses pulling at their bits, asked for their head. Not with words. No, Carothann's request wasn't even a thought, more like an unformed question wrapped up in the beginning of an idea.

Tamiel had buckled. Her breath came in gasps, and the demon stood, towering above her, fists in the air, ready to deal the deathblow.

"*No!*" Frankie cried.

Yes, Claire answered and let the tight control of her wand slip out of her hands.

A blast of magic poured out. She closed her eyes and let it tear through her. Instead of a caress, it rode wild and rough, but there was real power in its touch. The torrent of energy ripped the demon's side wide open.

With a thunderous roar, the beast whirled to Claire, clutching its side. Thick ooze poured out of the wound. In two bounds, it was on her.

She twisted away too late. The talons hooked her shoulder and dug in. Starbursts exploded behind her eyelids as a burning sensation attacked her upper back. Her legs left the ground as the beast pulled her toward it.

"Come on, Carth." Claire gritted her teeth. Together, she and Carothann were harnessing a power she had never felt before.

She shot the magic straight up into the demon's gut. It hit like a laser, and she dragged the beam with all her strength across its body, ripping a wide gash in its stomach. The beast howled, dropped Claire, and reared up on its haunches.

Tamiel jumped across the flaming crevice in a single bound and darted between them. Her blade struck the monster deep in the wound Claire had opened. Her hands hissed when they met with oozing flesh, and still, she pushed in deeper until her whole body shook with the effort.

Claire watched, dumbstruck, until her wand started writhing in her hand again. She let herself go, gave in to the magic, and pummeled the creature with everything she and Carothann had. Too much power. The tingling started in her belly and spread quickly to every nerve ending. She was on fire. Everything she knew screamed at her to drop the wand and run, but she hung on.

The monster roared, and suddenly, everything went black.

She came to before she opened her eyes. Something was jabbing at her. A poke on her shoulder, a nudge at her side. Tamiel? Frankie? What the hell was it?

Her mind was a haze. First things first. She shook her legs and then jostled her arms. Everything was still attached but hurt like a bitch. Her shoulder was a blazing ball of pain, and her forearm continued to burn raw.

She extended her senses beyond her own person. The room was strangely silent. Had they won or lost?

When she opened her eyes, the light hit them hard, and Tamiel came into view with a sudden sharpness. The angel's sunglasses were back in place, and she knelt beside Claire, peering down with a furrowed brow.

Frankie stood just behind, biting her bottom lip. "She okay?"

"I think so," Tamiel said. "Whoa, don't get up. It's over."

Claire sank back down. Sitting up hadn't been a good idea anyway. The light was too bright, and the room had started to spin the minute she raised her head.

More jabs in her side.

"Carothann?" she said with sudden recognition. "Where is it?" The wand was searching for her. Was it hurt? Something crazy had happened to it during the fight. That magic hadn't been standard FGC issue. "My wand?"

"Oh. We couldn't find it. I looked," Frankie said. "Maybe the demon got it."

"No, it's here. I can feel it." She pointed past Tamiel to the pile of boxes that had fallen from the shelf above. "There. Under that, maybe."

"I'll get it." Frankie started to the other side of the room.

"I'm closer." Tamiel moved in front of the girl, dug through the containers of powder detergent and dryer sheets, and found the wand under the bottom one.

Claire braced herself for Carothann's alarm at being touched. But nothing hit her. In fact, the wand lay peacefully in the angel's hand as if it belonged to her.

A few seconds later, Tamiel dropped the wand onto her palm. Carothann sank into her touch, burrowing in. Somehow they had survived the onslaught. She sat up and glanced around the empty room. The jagged crack still ran the entire length, but both fire and demons were long gone.

"What happened?" Claire asked.

"We got them."

"You saved me."

Tamiel and Frankie spoke at the same time.

Relief swept over Claire, and she gave a half laugh of disbelief.

"That was something. I had no idea you godmothers controlled that kind of magic," Tamiel said.

"Neither did I." Claire looked at the wand lying on her palm. It looked so unassuming, as if she had just randomly plucked a branch off a rowan tree on an afternoon walk. But something had happened to it and to her in that fight. Something revolutionary, if she could just figure out what it was.

"Is it...? Are they...coming back?" Frankie asked as if the thought had just occurred to her.

Claire looked at Tamiel for the answer.

The breeze that always blew around Tamiel died, and her body stiffened. "They answer to Yakum. I read it in that last one's eyes. Yakum's not going to give up."

"Who's Yakum?" Claire asked.

"Worst of the worst," Tamiel answered.

"There'll be more?" Frankie gasped and looked wildly around the room as if she expected the monsters to appear on the spot.

"Don't worry," Tamiel said before Claire could even fashion a response. "They come in threes, so we have time before he recruits another set."

"For what?" Frankie wrung her hands. "To figure out how to die? What if you hadn't been here? What if I had been alone?" Tears welled in her eyes.

She wasn't wrong. So many times, here and in the alley, the fight could've gone the other way. It almost had. Claire looked at her forearm; it was red and raw.

"You can't leave me alone." Frankie shuddered.

That much was true. Frankie had been unbelievably lucky that they had been here when the demons attacked. Carothann gave warning, of course, but the alarm system was built for a bad hookup in a frozen yogurt store, not a deadly creature from hell.

"Can you take me someplace protected? Like a place where there's more of you?" Frankie reached a hand out to Claire.

"Ouch!" They all focused on Claire's scalded forearm where Frankie's hand had dropped.

Frankie jerked it back immediately. "Oh God. I'm sorry. I—"

"No worries. No worries. We're all a little frazzled here."

Tears dropped from Frankie's eyes.

"Maybe there's someplace I could take you," Claire said, "that is a little more shielded."

Claire nodded to herself. There was, but Juliette wasn't going to like it at all.

Claire took a deep breath before she opened the door to the branch office. "Brace yourself. You're the first human to enter these doors in...maybe forever."

"These doors? Isn't this an abandoned building?" Frankie's voice still sounded shaky. She had calmed down considerably since their demon encounter, but she wouldn't stop wringing her hands. She had rushed Claire away from Tamiel as soon as Claire had laid out this crazy scheme. Before they'd had a chance to make plans to meet up again. Oh well, that was probably for the better.

"Not an abandoned building. Look." Claire pulled the doors open. The reception space was empty again. "Okay. You got me there. But there will be people in here." Claire slid her injured arm behind her back and led the way down the hall.

Everyone inside the staff room looked up the second they stepped through the door, and the hustle and bustle of the office died instantly.

"Who are all these people?" Frankie sucked in a quick breath as the rest of the office continued to stare.

"My colleagues waiting for their cases to be assigned. Other godmothers and godfathers. And that..." she pointed to Juliette, who stood in the doorway of her office, scowling. "... is my boss." The smooth, slow tone of her voice surprised the hell out of her. Inside, she was a bundle of nerves. Could she trade on all her years of exemplary service with the FGC for this huge misstep?

Juliette waved them over and quickly bustled them into her office. The muttering from the staff room began the instant the door closed. "What the hell, Claire!" The muscles around her mouth quivered. She was angrier than Claire had ever seen her.

"Funny you should use that terminology. Before I explain, though, Juliette, this is your charge, Frankie. Frankie, this is Juliette, my superior and co-godmother in this case."

"I have two godmothers?" Frankie's eyes went wide. "You have a wand too?"

Juliette raised the Manzanita branch as an answer before she grabbed Claire's good arm and dragged her to the far end of the desk. "I told you not to move further on this case until—" She shook her head and whispered, "What were you thinking?"

"Look." Claire twisted out of her grip. "You have no idea what it's like out there right now. Carothann's alarm went off. What else was I going to do?" Not exactly the whole truth, but she could get behind it.

"Stop talking. Not with her in here. Are you insane?" Juliette flicked her wand. An intercom's buzz filled the air. "Hugo, could you join us, please?"

After a few silent moments, the young apprentice appeared at the door. He looked back and forth between them, before blowing out his cheeks and releasing his breath with a pop. "Yes?"

"Hugo. This young human is Frankie. Would you be so kind as to take her into the break room and entertain her?"

Hugo glanced over at Claire, who nodded quickly. "You can tell her that story about the clothes designer who missed out on his Prince Charming when the two of you couldn't agree on his wardrobe."

Hugo nodded. "Oh, the day when a bolo tie ruined true love."

Claire was impressed he had gathered himself so quickly. Juliette's glare would make most people buckle at the knees. Claire grabbed Frankie's hands in hers and looked into the girl's eyes. "Could you go with Hugo? Just for a few minutes."

"I'd rather stay here with you." Frankie's shoulders started to curl over her chest. "I don't know him."

"You'll be safe. This place is like Fort Knox."

Hugo stepped up, slid his hand under Frankie's arm, and led her gently out of the room. "So my client wanted a bolo tie and..."

The second Hugo left, her heart started pounding. This was her third meeting with Administration in less than twenty-four hours, and while Juliette couldn't demote her on the spot, she did have the ears of Upper Administration who could. She glanced quickly to the case board. Her name still floated in curling, golden letters on two lines. But for how long?

The crazy thing was, she had done nothing wrong. But she knew the FGC was only about the end game. And this case was exploding all around her.

Juliette crossed her arms tightly over her chest and gave Claire a cold stare. "Okay. Now do you want to tell me why you brought our client in here?"

"Yes." She laid out her case in clear, even steps. She told Juliette everything—except when she got to the part about Carothann, a little voice in her head whispered, *Not that. I'll have to admit that I never took it to Wand Tech and that something is different. I don't even think there is a form for what happened today.*

So she glossed over how the wand had found a new gear in the heat of the battle and left it at, "Somehow, I found a way to defeat the demon."

Juliette said nothing at the story's end and simply rubbed her lips with the back of her fingers. "And how does the angel play into all of this?" she asked eventually.

"She's not after Frankie, if that's what you're asking. She had a bunch of chances to steal her from right under my nose, and she never made a move."

"She?"

"She presents as female more than anything else. I don't know why we ever called them *it*. That seems now to be shortsighted…"

When Juliette's brow began to furrow, she let her words drop. She needed to shut up. The prejudice ran deep, and this wasn't the time to buck the system or explore her own new feelings.

"You've done a pretty fast turnaround."

"I could be wrong." Claire raised her hands, trying to placate Juliette. Her gut, and her heart if she was being honest, were telling her that she wasn't. "And if Frankie's here, a place where demons would have trouble getting in, that frees me up to try to figure out what is really going on here. Unless you got the story from Upper Administration."

Juliette shook her head. "No. No one is admitting to generating the case. They're all passing the buck. That's why you shouldn't have brought her in here."

She's freaking out. She's afraid this whole case is going to come down on her head. Like Pierre. Claire needed to play this just right.

"If you have a better idea?" she backtracked. "Of course, I will do whatever you want."

"No. Leaving her here is good." She flicked Baltine. The conversation from the break room played in Juliette's office as if someone had switched on a speaker.

"And there was the case with the American actor who said he would never get married and the British lawyer who is all that. People think she was lucky to land him and that she was our client, but really it was the other way around. He just needed to see that he really wanted to get married. That's what a good godfather can do."

"You were responsible for that?" Frankie's voice rose in awe.

A pause, and then Hugo said, "Yes. That was my case."

"He wishes that was his case." Juliette rolled her eyes and grimaced. "He doesn't even have a wand yet."

"He just needs to distract her," Claire said loudly, trying to drown out whatever lie was flowing out of Hugo's mouth now. "It sounds like he's doing a pretty good job of that."

Juliette flicked her wand, and the conversation cut out. "Okay. This is what we're going to do. Leave her here with me. You go to Medical. Now. You're dripping blood all over my carpet."

Claire glanced down. Sure enough. A few beads of red stained the carpet. Her shoulder and arm throbbed.

"Okay," she said quickly. Getting out of there without a demotion had seemed like a long shot when she'd walked in.

"I'll get in touch with you first thing tomorrow morning and tell you how to proceed. Do not contact the angel or investigate on your own. Got it?"

Claire nodded.

"I'm serious, Claire. Upper Administration isn't happy that you're on a case no one has approved."

Claire swallowed hard. It wasn't as if she had procured the case by herself. When had *we* turned into *you*?

"You understand? Sit tight at home."

"I do." Easy to say. She didn't even know how to get in contact with Tamiel. But the thought of not seeing the angel again sent a strange tightness into her chest. She glanced down quickly, wondering if she had given her feelings away, but Juliette, lost in her own problems, was tapping her fingers on her desk.

"Let me just say good-bye to Frankie, then."

"What? Frankie? No. Let's not get her riled up. She's good with Hugo, and I'll get some burgers and keep her entertained for the night. Maybe some charades. She's an actress, right?"

"An artist. And eighteen, not six."

"Oh, even better. There are some colored pencils, I think, in the storeroom. And you?" She turned all her attention to Claire and pointed out of the office. "Off to Medical and then Filing. You're way overdue on your forms."

Claire would have darted into the staff room to say good-bye to Frankie anyway, but Juliette walked her down the hallway to Medical as if she were escorting a prisoner to execution. Her mouth was pressed into a hard line, and she pointed to the elderly woman in the back of the room before she hightailed it back down the hall.

"You hurt, dear?" the retired godmother who was now a nurse asked.

Claire nodded, even started to point to her shoulder, when a thought hit her loud and clear.

I don't want to go to Medical. I want to go home.

It had just jumped into her mind. The actual treatment was quick, but the forms would take forever, especially on a case that had no clear origin stamp. And she wanted to go home to examine Carothann away from the watchful eye of Juliette. To figure out what on earth had happened to it at Frankie's. She could come back tomorrow if either her shoulder or her arm still hurt and to fill out the inevitable forms all the magic at Frankie's and Abby's would require.

"Oh good. You got my message." Tamiel bounced up from the sofa and rushed to Claire as soon as she materialized in her own living room.

"What message?" Claire took a startled step back, but her heartbeat quickened at the sight of the angel by her coffee table.

"The *come home* one."

Claire frowned and thought back to the moment she had decided to skip Medical. "That was you?" The old prejudices and a hundred cautionary tales about angel mind control came rushing back. She did not like the idea of the angel, or anyone for that matter, in her head

"Yeah, sorry. I don't normally send out those kinds of messages. Not on you anyhow." Tamiel bounced on her feet. "But I'm just excited. Usually, I have to stay completely glamoured when I'm out in the field. This," she waved a hand between them, "is a new experience for me."

"Can I ask you not to do that?"

Tamiel's brow furrowed. "Do what?"

"I need to know when my thoughts aren't my own."

"Oh, okay. Sorry." Red washed over Tamiel's cheeks and down her neck.

Angels can blush? It was completely endearing, and Claire's annoyance faded as quickly as it had risen.

"No, it's just that—"

"I don't have a lot—"

They'd both started speaking at the same time and then stopped at the same time.

"Sorry," Tamiel said again and tapped her fingers on her leg.

"No, you first."

"I was saying I don't have a lot of experience. Face-to-face experience, that is. I mean, I've been doing this for ages..."

Obviously. Tamiel's fighting and slashing the demons had really been something.

"But, boy, do I envy you guys. Being able to interact with your clients whenever you want."

Wow, the GA was jealous of the FGC! Claire hadn't seen that coming. "Believe me, it's not all it's cracked up to be."

They both stood in silence. Tamiel's fingers were still going a mile a minute.

"Hey, what about all the angel sightings?" Claire cast around for a subject that wasn't quite as personal. "You guys seem to be all over the place."

"I know." Tamiel spread out her fingers and stopped the drumming. She laughed and music filled the air. "That's mostly Agla, though. Once he saved Lot from Sodom and Gomorrah, he got a taste for being the hero. Now he can't stop himself. He warns people about earthquakes, tornadoes, cups falling off shelves. He's everywhere. I can help you with that, you know."

"With what?"

"Your shoulder and your arm. And whatever else is hurting you."

Claire's hand froze on her neck. She hadn't been aware she was rubbing it.

"I'm okay," she said, quickly dropping her gaze and pulling her hand away. The easy conversation hadn't lasted long.

"No, seriously. It won't take but a minute. There's no reason for you to be in pain. That's one of the reasons I called you home, actually."

"Okay." Claire should say no and find any excuse for Tamiel to leave. All the stories she had ever heard as a kid and all the FGC workshops had told her this—whatever *this* was—was a horrible idea for so many reasons. And yet, from the second Tamiel had leaped off the sofa, she had been aware of her—the adorable way she tilted her head when she was nervous, the fresh pine and lavender in the air, the energy that seemed to drag her closer as if they were dual stars orbiting each other.

Claire went still as Tamiel slid her sunglasses to the coffee table and moved to her side. She glanced into the angel's eyes.

The burning flames were not the raging inferno of battle. Instead, their heat was warm and comforting again, like a hearth on a cold day. She was so close. All Claire had to do was raise her hand and they would be touching. The thought had barely taken root before Tamiel moved around to her back. Tamiel's gentle breath circled her neck, and Claire licked her lips, waiting for her fingers to follow. The touch in the alley, although brief, had been so soft. What would this one be like?

Her fluttering nerves turned jagged as nothing happened.

"Um… I don't know… I think your top might be stuck."

Claire closed her eyes and swallowed hard. "On what?"

"The wound. The demon did a real number on you. The blood and the top. They've all kind of dried together into a big mess."

She chewed on her bottom lip. The encounter had started with such promise.

"Maybe I can take it off," Tamiel said.

Claire's heart jumped.

"Or at least the sleeve and these parts around here."

Claire had no idea what she was pointing to, and if she agreed, she might be half-naked in under a second. That was a little quick in her book. The fluttering in her belly, however, urged her forward.

"Okay," she said. Excitement and fear surged through her veins. Tamiel's concern might just be the kindness of angels. Who knew if they even had relationships? But Claire had sensed an energy that was electric between them since…the alley, really. That had to mean something.

Claire's top down to her bra disappeared with a soft whoosh, and she stopped thinking. Tamiel's fingers caressed the wound. Knitting it back together, making it whole. Pain flared at the first brush, but then an energy glowing with heat pulsated through her body and spread beyond her shoulder. The pain faded as Claire concentrated on Tamiel's touch. Her fingers moved in small circles, targeting separately each gash the demon's talons had made. Then her hands seemed to be everywhere, running lightly down her back, sliding up and over her shoulder, dipping down her front. One hand lingered oh so close to her breast while the other kneaded the tightness out of her neck.

Claire licked her lips. She was acutely aware of every spot Tamiel's fingers roamed. And then she zeroed in on that one hand, resting just above her breast. Only an inch would transform this healing into… Muscles below her belly clenched as a slow wave of excitement rode through her.

This feels too good. I shouldn't… I shouldn't… I can't help it…

Just as she gave in to the feeling, the warmth coursing through her body shifted to coolness and then to nothing. Tamiel's fingers lifted off her shoulder.

"Better?" Tamiel asked as she took a step back.

Claire felt the loss of the angel's touch to her toes. She breathed in deeply, trying to find her equilibrium again.

"Yes." She managed to choke out the answer. She swung her shoulder around, just to give herself something to do. Wow. Flexible and fluid. That crick she'd had in her neck since she moved heaven and earth for Grace Kelly to become Princess of Monaco was completely gone. Tamiel had worked miracles.

I guess that's what they do.

"From back here it looks like it never happened."

Claire wished she could read Tamiel's tone. She spun a little on one heel and then shifted to the toes of her other foot, buying time. She raised her head to meet the angel's gaze. They connected. The flames leaped up in Tamiel's irises, and the breath caught in her throat.

They were barely a step apart. Kinetic energy whirled around them, pushing them together. It would be so easy to step into the force and let it envelop her. Wrap her arms around Tamiel and raise her lips to the angel's. She imagined that healing, wonderful touch on her mouth and almost went weak at the knees.

But she did nothing.

Shyness, uncertainty, and a particularly vehement lecture on angel mind control from a weekend workshop in Palm Springs rooted her to the floor. The energy died, and they were just two magical creatures standing by a faux leather sofa from IKEA.

"Oh, sorry. I forgot your top." Tamiel took another step back, and cloth spread over Claire's shoulder in a flash. "So what happened when you reported in?"

Claire let out a long breath.

"You can trust me. Whatever this is, we're in it together."

No, that's not why I'm sighing.

Tamiel tilted her head first to one side and then the other, waiting for an answer.

"My boss is taking Frankie for the night and probably throwing me under the bus with Upper Administration. But the real kicker is that no one in the FGC knows where this case came from."

"Interesting."

"No kidding. What do your superiors say?"

"We don't have superiors. I mean, there is a hierarchy, of course; everyone knows that." She raised her hands and shrugged. "I'm happily at the bottom in the lowest choir. Off anyone's radar. But with the whole cosmos under our domain, even the big guns are pretty much left to their own devices in the field."

"Wow. I can't even imagine."

"I hope you never have to. It gets pretty lonely," Tamiel said and sat on the couch. "So no one at the FGC is asking why this girl is being attacked by demons?"

"No." The impact of that statement hit Claire squarely in the gut. She had been so worried about retaining her job and dodging all the directives about Wand Tech, Medical, and Filing that this particular subject had never come up. Wow, she was no better than Juliette. "No, no one is asking."

"I'll tell you what I think." Tamiel leaned back into the sofa. "That there is more to this case than meets the eye. Sure, demons attack all the time. They are responsible for a lot of the terrible things that happen in the world. But the fact these demons come from Yakum makes this a whole new ball game."

"Why?"

"Long story."

"I'm ready." She dropped onto the couch near Tamiel. Thank goodness, the angel seemed to be staying.

"Yakum is the worst kind of angel—"

"Angel? I thought you said he was a demon."

"No, I said he sent out demons."

"You guys can do that?" Claire's mind whirled.

"The GA is very complicated, and the answer's much more fluid than a simple yes or no."

"Try me."

Tamiel rubbed the back of her neck. "Okay. Basically, Yakum started out as a Grigori or a Watcher. That's the same choir as me, but not the same level. He's stronger. Much stronger. And yet, strangely, Watchers do a lot of what lower Guardians do.

They look out for humans, appear to them in dreams, and give advice, but with Yakum, it went horribly wrong."

"How?"

"Personally, I think he enjoyed the power he had over the humans he was caring for. Like I said, this gig is sometimes really lonely, but that doesn't excuse what he did." She took Claire's hand.

Adrenaline pulsed through Claire's veins as her heart leaped in her chest. What was Tamiel doing? She glanced down. Tamiel intertwined her fingers with Claire's to hold her still and then ran her other hand with featherlight touches up Claire's burned forearm. Claire willed her heart to slow. This was all part of the service. Tamiel didn't mean anything else by it. The skin on her arm turned slowly pink and then white under Tamiel's touch as the healing energy buzzed through it. Not fair. How was she supposed to concentrate?

Claire jerked her head up to the angel's face. Watching the fire dance in her eyes and her mouth move wasn't much easier.

"Yakum was really smart about how he connected with the humans. He started out small with gifts of mirrors and cosmetics. Just to get them hooked. And then he moved on to knives and swords and the killing blows those weapons could yield. Sometimes he even went as far as teaching them enchantments and sorcery."

Moving again in small circles, Tamiel caressed a particularly tender spot.

"Ooh." Claire tried to bite back the moan before it was all the way out.

"Yeah, right here's pretty bad." Tamiel smiled softly, and Claire's heart did another flip-flop.

"Anyway, one day, apparently, he was watching over this beautiful young girl in Samaria, and he appeared to her with, you know, the kinds of gifts that would get her attention. Abal was her name, I think. He was tall and handsome, and the fire rose in his eyes with kindness. One look in those eyes and she was his."

Or maybe he ran his fingers up and down her arm.

"In the beginning, Yakum was everything Abal had ever dreamed of. Attentive, loving, generous, and before she knew it, they were spending every waking moment together. Pretty soon the whole town started to gossip about her and the mysterious stranger and her immodest behavior. This was Samaria in the Iron Age after all, and before long, the talk got so bad that the whole town stopped buying grain from her uncle. His business—the one he had stolen from Abal's father, by the way—started to fail. The uncle, of course, blamed Abal."

Claire shook her head. "The girl's always the scapegoat. I can't tell you how many times I've seen that from my end too."

Tamiel nodded. "It's an easy way not to take responsibility. Abal's uncle tried to lock her up in a tiny room in the back of the house. But each time, as soon as the key turned in the lock, she would vanish. Yakum's magic was very strong. But, of course, the uncle didn't know that. He only knew that Abal, despite his very best efforts, was disappearing and making a royal fool of him in front of the whole village. The uncle got madder and madder each time it happened, and soon, he was fit to be tied."

Tamiel flipped Claire's arm, and her fingers slid delicately down its underside. Chills spread to every part of Claire's body.

"And…" Tamiel took a deep, strategic breath. "Brace yourself. One night as Abal was sleeping, the uncle crept into her room. He meant to beat her so badly that she would no longer be pretty. He thought if he did, Yakum wouldn't want

71

her and he could rebuild the business and his own reputation. But the moment the uncle raised his cane to strike the first blow, a great, flaming light burned through the room. Yakum stepped right out of that fire. He raised a long finger at the uncle and cried, 'Judgment has come,' and slammed a fireball into him. The uncle crumpled to the ground. Instantly dead and never able to hurt anyone ever again. When the fireball dissipated, Abal readied herself to see a horribly burned corpse. Instead, she gasped at what lay before her."

"What? What did she see?" Claire leaned in closer. Her arm was almost in Tamiel's lap.

"Her uncle's body was fine. His face, however, was all black and blue and beaten almost to a pulp. She raised her hands and screamed, only to find she was holding the very same cane the uncle had carried into her room. And that's how her cousin found her. Standing over the beaten, dead body of his own father, clutching the murder weapon. This time, there was no escape for Abal."

Tamiel's fingers froze on Claire's arm as Abal's dire predicament spread out all around them.

"That was the plan all along. Wasn't it?"

"Yep." Tamiel smiled grimly and started up again. She stretched Claire's fingers wide with one hand and rubbed her open palm with the other. This time, Claire found the willpower to suppress the groan.

"Yes, her cousin was ready to kill Abal right then and there. In fact, when his mother and sisters came skidding into the room only seconds later, he already had Abal up against the wall and by the throat. He was so consumed by his righteous anger and hatred that he didn't even see the huge, dark Watcher standing by his cousin's side. But Yakum noticed everything.

He turned to Abal and said, 'Choose. Your fate with him or your fate with me.'"

"Oh man."

"There was no choice, really. Either she could die horribly at the hands of her cousin right then and there or take her chances with Yakum, who eventually did much, much worse."

"That's not much of a choice."

"No. Obviously, you know where I'm going with this. He lay with her, against her will. Over and over again until she was broken.

"Yakum left the girl with child, and when her son was born, he was a monster both inside and out. The boy was big and strong. And he obeyed his father faithfully. Yakum saw the potential in what he had created in Abal. He wanted power. And for that, he needed an army of his own children. He didn't care what he had to give up to get it."

Claire glanced down at her hand. Tamiel had stopped rubbing, and her hand sat in Claire's like a lover's. Tamiel pulled away.

"So that's what he wants with Frankie?" Claire asked softly, tamping down the desire to grab the angel's hand back.

"If I had to guess, I'd say yes."

"Why her? There're a million other women out there."

Tamiel shrugged. "I don't know."

They sat in in silence for a long moment. Claire found her voice first. "So what do we do?"

She knew what she should do. Rush back to Juliette and let the FGC know what they were dealing with. But Claire didn't even get up. The FGC's hold was beginning to loosen. Their path wasn't the only one. She settled back into the couch, telling herself she just wanted to hear what the angel would say.

"Get Yakum. If we don't stop him, then Frankie and who knows who else will be in danger."

Tamiel's certainty tugged at Claire. "You make it sound so simple."

"It's not without danger, of course, but we can't let Yakum take her. I have a plan. And you, apparently, have a secret weapon."

"What?"

"Your wand. Caroman."

"Carothann." Cute how she got it wrong. The mispronunciation from anyone else would have irked Claire.

"Carothann," Tamiel repeated and leaned back into the cushions. "So what's going on? I've never seen magic that powerful from the FGC."

"I don't know. It's never acted like that before." She produced Carothann from her inside pocket and held it in her palm. Small currents of magic buzzed around it, lighting up various portions of the wand in a golden glow, but otherwise, it looked and felt completely normal—right down to Frankie and Abby's bands sitting at the bottom of the branch.

Shit, Abby. Claire had completely forgotten about her. She hoped she was okay.

"So you need that, right?" For a moment she thought Tamiel meant Abby. She needed Abby like a hole in the head, but Tamiel pointed to Carothann. "You can't engage the magic unless you have a wand?"

"No. Not even a little bit."

Tamiel nodded. "That's right. It totally makes sense. You're part human, right?"

"Yeah."

"And the other part?"

"No one knows. A whole bunch of us just popped up in France four centuries ago. And then someone leaked the story of Cinderella to that French author Charles Perrault, although I can't tell you how many facts he got wrong, and we were outed. The name totally kills us, though. We couldn't have less in common with fairies, and these days it's super hard to be a godmother to some of these spoiled girls." Claire bit her lip, realizing she was beginning to ramble. Silence hung in the air between them.

"So where do the wands come from?"

"If you become an apprentice, you get to go to the head office in Paris. You walk in and a wand calls to you."

"So that's the only place?"

"Yeah, I mean, there're rumors that there're wands out in the wild that call to the truly deserving. But I've never actually met anyone that's happened to."

"What makes someone deserving?"

Claire shrugged. "I'm the last person to ask."

Silence filled the room. Tamiel reached out her hand just shy of Carothann. "May I?"

Claire hesitated. She had just divulged some of the FGC's innermost secrets, and this could be the end game of an elaborate ploy. But Carothann had trusted her earlier. It was the best judge of character she knew. So, for reasons she didn't entirely understand herself, she dropped the wand into the angel's hand.

Just like earlier in Frankie's room, Carothann didn't buck or spark. It just lay there as if nothing were wrong.

"Oh, now I see." Tamiel stared at the wand. "The FGC constricts the magic with a filter. Mmm. Doesn't that cut you off at the knees in the field?"

"There's no filter on it." Confusion and indignation rose in her. She snatched it back.

"Yes, there is." She pointed near the top. "Right about here. Surely you feel it straining sometimes?"

She had, but she didn't want to admit Tamiel knew her wand better than she did.

"Look. You don't have to tell me anything."

Claire stared at the spot Tamiel had been pointing to. She saw nothing.

"I get that there's this thing," Tamiel waved her hand back and forth, "between our organizations—at least from your side. And you can keep to yourself whatever you want. But you did know, right?"

Claire struggled only for an instant. "No, I didn't know." And then, "Are you sure?"

"I'm sorry."

"Yeah, me too."

"Maybe there is a reason," Tamiel said.

"Maybe." But what, Claire couldn't fathom.

"When did yours break?" Tamiel didn't wait for an answer. "Your filter, it's broken. This explains what happened at Frankie's. You were on full power. Was that the first time?"

"Yes. There sure was something different about it and us." Claire pushed the betrayal she was feeling from the FGC into a little compartment in her mind to deal with later. "Usually, it just receives and amplifies my thoughts, but for the first time I felt like we were a real team, and it was more than a tool."

"See, we can use that to our advantage. You have a mighty weapon there, and the only demons who can reveal that are dead." Tamiel ran a finger down the shaft, and it lifted ever so slightly to meet her touch.

Oh God, not you too. Down there, Carth.

"It's pretty special."

"It's weird." Claire shook her head. "It doesn't usually take to anyone else."

"I told you. I'm good folk."

A thousand contradictory thoughts swirled in Claire's mind. But she trusted Carothann with a bond that soared beyond thoughts.

"Maybe you are."

"That wasn't so hard, was it?"

"What?"

"Pushing aside other people's truths. There's more out there than what the FGC tells you. But I'm not about to start doing the same thing. Controlling your magic or telling you what to think and all." She leaped from the couch. "Do you need to eat or to sleep? I don't do either, and sometimes I find these schedules very confusing."

At the mention of eating, Claire's stomach rumbled. "Yes, both."

"All right, let's get you fed and then into bed."

Heat rose to Claire's cheeks, but Tamiel clearly hadn't meant anything risqué by it. She was bounding into the kitchen and calling over her shoulder, "We have a big day tomorrow. You need to be well rested."

Claire followed but stopped at the door. Actually, she was more tired than hungry. It had been quite the day. Two battles, a healing touch, the revelation about Carothann. Too much to take in. Tamiel was right; she needed to eat something and go to bed. "What will you do while I sleep?"

Tamiel had her hands in the fridge. Clinking noises followed as her head bobbed up and down. "What I always do. Watch over my charge."

Dang. So she wasn't staying.

Tamiel popped out with a green apple in her hand and cut into Claire's thoughts. "This looks good." She had almost dropped it into Claire's hand when she snatched it back. "Or should it be red? Is this one bad?"

"No." Claire smiled and reached out for the apple. "They're good in both colors."

"Just like the truth. It comes in all sorts of colors too."

Claire nodded, although apples were a lot different than a lifetime of knowledge shoved into her by the FGC.

But this she did know. Twenty-four hours ago, the idea of an angel in her home rummaging through her fridge would have given her the heebie-jeebies, to say the least.

Now Tamiel stood in the kitchen with that goofy smile on her face as she watched Claire sink her teeth into the crisp fruit. Maybe Tamiel was right. The GA and the FGC were like apples. There were red ones and green ones. Different flavors of help.

One just as good as the other.

CHAPTER 4

One Day Earlier

HEAVY KNOCKING POUNDED INTO CLAIRE'S dreams. Someone was hammering on the front door super hard. "Claire? Level-one-plus? Are you in there? Can you hear me?"

She jumped out of bed. "Hang on. Hang on. Who is it?"

"Hugo. Level-ten-minus." The apprentice who had taken Frankie. Was something wrong?

Claire hurried through the living room, rubbing the sleep from her eyes. From the moment she had said good night to Tamiel and her head hit the pillow, she had, surprisingly, slept like a baby, dead to the world. She looked around. Had the angel come back?

No, the living room was empty. Her heart sank, but it was probably better if Tamiel wasn't by her side when she greeted the apprentice.

Hugo shuffled in the doorway, clearly unsure what to do next. "Oh, I'm so sorry, Ms. Claire, were you sleeping?"

"Is everything okay with Frankie?"

"Yes. She's fine."

Claire pressed a palm to her heart. "So why are you here?"

"Oh, Juliette has been trying to get a hold of you all morning. Didn't Carothann tell you?"

"No." She pulled her wand out from the pocket of magic at her side. She had decided at the last minute last night to keep it with her rather than let it rest in its box. "It's been acting up lately. I need to get it in to Wand Tech," she said but silently vowed never to let the FGC touch it again.

"Yeah. She said that must be it. When she couldn't get a hold of you, she sent me. Get dressed. She's waiting—" Hugo jumped back, squeezed his eyes shut, and popped them open as he gazed past Claire.

She turned, although she already knew what had startled him.

Once again, Tamiel must have stepped into existence— from out of thin air to two feet away.

"Don't look at it!" He jerked his head down. "It's an angel!"

"It's all right. They're not like that." Claire turned to Tamiel and smiled. "You came back?"

"Yes."

"You know it?" Hugo's eyes went round as he raised his head and took them both in.

"I do. She's okay."

Hugo glanced back and forth between them. "Juliette needs you back at the office." His tone hardened. "Immediately."

"No," Tamiel said, her voice just as steely. "We need to go after Yakum."

Claire took a deep breath and held it tight. Defending an angel to an apprentice was one thing. Running off with her against a direct order from an FGC operative was something else entirely.

Hugo and Tamiel stared at her, waiting for her decision. She let the panic run its course as her mind coalesced around the only thing that really mattered. What was best for Frankie here? Certainly not falling into Yakum's claws or sitting in Beverly Hills doing one load of laundry after another or even hiding out at the FGC for the rest of her life. Frankie deserved her happily ever after. But FGC or GA? Status quo or take a chance? The decision could change the rest of her life. She froze as she saw herself going both ways in her mind's eye.

Carothann twitched in her hand. It jerked toward Tamiel, clearly pushing her in that direction. It knew somehow, and if she was being honest, she knew too. She gave Carothann a gentle squeeze of trust and thanks.

"Okay. I'm with you." She swiveled to face Tamiel.

"You're kidding? What am I supposed to tell Juliette?"

Good question. She had no idea how all of this was going to play out, but she did feel sorry for Hugo. Life was hard for an apprentice, especially a male one, at the FGC. "Tell her I wasn't here. Knock again in a minute and it will actually be true." She closed the door softly in his face.

"Come on." She slid an arm under Tamiel's—fought down the fluttering below her belly at the contact—and pulled her into the middle of the room. "You said last night you had a plan?"

"The demon's here?" Claire raised an eyebrow.

Tamiel nodded. "Technically, Yakum is a fallen angel. Demons have no souls and can be conscripted to action—two completely different species. But yes, he's here. Why?"

Claire glanced around the brightly painted room flush with display cases and cartoonish lettering on the walls.

"Because this is a Real or Not Real Emporium. You know this place?"

"No."

"Well, it's either a warehouse full of odd and unnatural things from all over the world. Or it's a tourist trap in the middle of Hollywood."

"Oh, I get it. Real or not real." Tamiel smiled thinly. "That's so smart."

Claire threw her a questioning glance.

"You think the FGC invented hiding in plain sight? This is the perfect place for Yakum. Read it." Tamiel pointed to a life-size statue right in front of them and the plaque at its bottom.

"Did Black Mamba Man," Claire read out loud, "just tattoo the silver-gray pattern on his face and file his teeth? Or is he really half snake? You be the judge. Real or not real?"

Tamiel snorted. "Anyone who's met Black Mamba on a dark night will tell you his teeth are not filed. They are naturally that razor-sharp."

"You're saying he's real?" If she were a betting woman, Claire would have put Black Mamba and his forked tongue firmly in the *not real* category.

"Yeah. That's one of Yakum's children. Think about it. It's diabolically clever. He has this place so he can desensitize the world to his children. They get publicity here as weirdoes, not supernatural hybrids. When humans run into them, they're not scared. And Black Mamba and all his brothers and sisters have free rein."

"To do what?"

"No one's quite sure. But it can't be good."

"What about that human pincushion guy?" Claire turned to a picture of a man on the wall behind Black Mamba. Safety and straight-edge pins pierced almost every square inch of his skin. He stared out of the photo with glowing, yellow eyes that up until a minute ago Claire would have sworn were a crazy pair of contacts.

"Yeah, him too. But he's not much of a threat. He's always stopping to stick the pins back in. They pop out all the time."

"That's just not right." Claire shook her head. Her world had been so ordered before Tamiel. Sure, boring as hell, but predictable. Now everything she thought she knew was being turned on its head.

"What does Yakum look like?" She envisioned a combination of all the weirdest people she had ever seen.

"I've never met him. Just heard the stories that drift around. But I can target where he is. We all can if the angel is in our choir. Normally, we just don't use the ability."

She headed off, but Claire couldn't take her eyes off the pictures and statues of the strange new reality all around her.

"Come on. The entrance to his lair is back over here."

Tamiel walked away with a steady step.

Following her could easily be one of those things there was no coming back from. But, if anything, the last two days had taught Claire that standing still wasn't an option either. She had been practically strapped into a straightjacket at work lately. Letting Abby's Prince Charming run off with another girl had been as much about finding a missing purpose in her work as true love.

Tamiel disappeared around the corner. Claire took a deep breath and entered into a room plastered with portraits of celebrities fashioned from gumdrops. Real, but shouldn't be.

Tamiel stood at the far side by a door marked *EMPLOYEES ONLY*, her hand already on its handle. She twisted back to Claire as soon as she caught up. "Ready?"

Claire nodded although the heat rising from her chest told her she probably wasn't.

Tamiel opened the door with a lurch, and suddenly it was a whole new ball game.

The colorful museum gave way to a long hall that slopped eternally downward. Dark stone walls and low lighting made the passageway almost claustrophobic, but strangely, the new surroundings comforted Claire. This was what a demon lair was supposed to look like. No, wait, he was a fallen angel, not a demon. Could she ever get rid of her preconceptions?

Every so often the walls dipped into a nook, a perfect hiding place, and Claire pulled Carothann out of its pocket just in case.

It shivered and jumped in her hand, thrilled, Claire guessed, to be released from the magic pocket. She liked this new Carothann. She loved its responsiveness and the growing connection between them. Whatever happened here, she was pretty sure she couldn't go back to a wand with a filter.

"How do you know where you're going?" she asked.

"The smell."

Claire sniffed the air. "I don't smell anything."

"You will." And she kept on walking down the unending hallway.

The smell came at Claire slowly. Tickling her nose first with the scent of rotten meat and sulfur. She coughed and gagged as the odor turned sour, as if animals had crawled into the walls and died.

"What is that?" Claire asked, holding her hand up to her nose.

"The smell of bad choices." Tamiel turned to her and waved a hand. The fresh mountain breeze, always swirling around her, surged through the tunnel, and Claire dropped her hand.

"Thanks," she said.

"Get ready. We're close."

They rounded a corner and dead-ended at a large wooden door built into the stone wall. Rusted iron straps and bolts fastened together thick wooden planks, and it looked as if it had been standing there since the beginning of time.

"There could be hellhounds," Tamiel said softly in the quiet before the storm.

"Okay." But Claire had no idea what to expect. There were never any hellhounds in birth blessings and makeovers. Her hands, especially the one clutched around Carothann, began to tremble. She fought down the surging impulse to race back to the museum. "Look. You need to tell me what to do and when," she said instead, putting her future squarely in Tamiel's hands.

"Yes, but go with your instincts. They're good." Tamiel gave her a smile. "We make a very good team."

The flames inside Tamiel's eyes surged as Claire met her gaze. Any other time, such a look would have sent butterflies soaring in her belly, but the adrenaline rushing through her veins kept them at bay.

"Here we go." Tamiel pulled her sword from the scabbard on her back and pointed it at the door. Flame leaped from its tip and bored into the keyhole. The door swung open with a creak worthy of any haunted house.

Inside, two canine-like creatures, all legs and muscle, raced toward them down another dark corridor, their sharp teeth bared. Snarls echoed off the walls. They were fast, but Tamiel was faster. She was on them with astonishing speed and brought her sword up and down in a blur of flame.

The blow crashed down on the hellhound in front but did little to stop it. Roaring with fury, it lashed out with its teeth, but Tamiel had already bounded up and over the creature, yanking her knees up out of its reach. The hound twisted while she was in the air and snapped, missing only by inches.

All yours. She threw the thought into Claire's head. Finally, some direction! Claire blasted the creature with a shot from her wand. The hellhounds yelped, but her attack did little harm. Just as the one in front rocked back onto its hind legs, ready to pounce, a shout came out of the darkness.

"Sit!"

Both beasts went down on their haunches.

"Heel." The hellhounds, which had been snarling monsters just seconds before, retreated, trotting down the rest of the long hallway as if they were promenading in a dog show.

Claire peered into the darkness, but she could only make out a tall shape at the end of the corridor.

"Sorry. They're just for appearances. Not quite the welcome I was going for."

"Yakum?"

"The one and only. Nice to meet you, Tamiel. And you too, Claire." With a hellhound on either side, he walked forward into the dim light.

Claire gasped. He looked so much like Tamiel. The only difference was in the way they were dressed. Instead of liquid silver, Yakum sported a finely tailored suit that hugged a similar wiry body. His lovely features read only slightly more male than female. But his eyes struck Claire like a slap. They were Tamiel's eyes—deep, luminous, and filled with the exact same fire. *Mother Chimera.*

She jerked her head away. Had he met her glance? Was this a trap? Was she glamoured? Would she even know? She didn't feel any different—still like herself.

But who knew. She was in way over her head.

"What took you so long?" Yakum's pitch was low and musical. Even his voice resembled Tamiel's. "Come, come." He ushered them down the hall.

Claire didn't move. She had imagined this attack playing out very differently. Certainly not as a leisurely stroll with a fallen angel and a couple of hellhounds.

Yakum waved to Tamiel, who also had frozen. "Please. I've been waiting a long time for this moment, cousin."

They're cousins! Claire flinched. This was a trap!

No. Tamiel's voice sprang up in her head even before her thought was complete. *We don't know each other. We're just in the same choir. We're all cousins.*

Claire threw a questioning look at Tamiel. Shit. Was the angel reading her mind now? At this moment, though, Tamiel's closeness was her only lifeline in this gigantic mess.

It's going to be okay. Tamiel followed Yakum but, despite her words, didn't sheath her sword. When she passed, she squeezed Claire's arm with her free hand.

Just a fleeting touch, but calm flooded her body. Suddenly, a meeting with Yakum didn't seem like the worst idea in the world. Nice. She needed that. On the other hand, she'd make the exact same move if she had a client who wasn't behaving. *If I had powers like hers, that is.*

Claire glanced at the wooden door behind her. Leaving now was the smart move. But where would she go once the door shut behind her? Not the FGC.

This *was* a trap! It was just a snare of her own making. She had laid the groundwork with all her blatant infractions over the last two days. Now, she could only move forward. Claire tightened her grip on Carothann and forced her feet down the hall.

The corridor opened into a large, circular stone room. The walls rose into a dome, and it was furnished with heavy wooden furniture. Chairs, a table, and wardrobes filled the space around a giant hearth where a blue fire blazed.

Claire sniffed the air. Gone was the hideous stink. Unbelievably, now it smelled like a citrus grove.

"Yeah," Yakum said as he made his way to a throne-like chair against one of the curves of the wall, "the smell is just a diversionary tactic. Don't want any unwelcome visitors." The beasts padded over with him. One even put its muzzle, the size of a football, on Yakum's knee when he sat down.

"Sit, sit." He pointed to two padded chairs nearby.

"Thanks, we're good," Tamiel said.

Be careful. The thought popped into Claire's head. *He's a wily one.*

She shook her head to clear it of Tamiel's influence. Forget what everybody else thought. Time to think for herself!

She studied Yakum. He didn't look slippery or evil. In fact, fine worry lines surrounded his eyes, and there had been the slightest shuffle to his step as he crossed the room. Actually, he just looked tired. Was that part of the ruse?

"Yakum, we're here to stop you from killing Frankie," Tamiel said.

Notes almost like bassoons and cellos filled the air. He laughed musically, just like Tamiel. Although this laugh was in a minor key, almost a sad melody. "You got it all wrong, Tamiel. Like they always do up there."

Tamiel flicked her gaze upward and sighed heavily. "Why don't you enlighten us, Yakum?"

Claire bit her lip. Again, this wasn't at all how she had thought it would go down. She thought they would race in,

Tamiel's sword ablaze, Carothann at full power, and destroy whatever and whoever was in this chamber. Good would win, Frankie would be free of the crushing evil surrounding her, and finally Claire could close her case.

Instead, Yakum and Tamiel were throwing barbs at each other like siblings at an awkward family reunion. This, whatever *this* was, was…anticlimactic.

"You're after the wrong culprit." Yakum smiled thinly.

Tamiel leveled a glassy stare straight at him. "Really?"

"Yes. The one who's causing all this trouble is…" He paused and rubbed his hands in dramatic effect. "…Francesca."

"What?" Tamiel and Claire echoed each other.

Tamiel jumped at him, her sword blazing hot in a nanosecond.

Yakum held up a delicate hand. "Hear me out."

Sword aloft, Tamiel trembled. The tendons in her neck throbbed as she fought to gain control. "No games," she said finally between clenched teeth.

He threw the other hand up as well. "Of course. But this will go better if you put away the sword."

Tamiel lowered her weapon, and the flame died along its edge.

"Away," Yakum repeated.

"This is all you're getting. Now talk."

"Okay. Brace yourself. Francesca may look human. She got that from her mother, the lovely creature that she was. But believe me, inside that girl is all fallen angel. And not the good kind."

"There's a good kind of fallen angel?" Claire found her voice.

"Of course. There's always good and bad in everything. Nature tries to maintain a balance of some sort. Don't they teach you anything at the FGC?" He didn't wait for an answer. "I don't even know where she got the bad from. Certainly not me."

Tamiel's head dropped to her chest.

Claire shook hers. "From you?"

"A little dim, this one?" He flicked his finger at Claire.

"No. Just inexperienced." Tamiel met her gaze. "He doesn't want Frankie as a breeder. He's already done that. She's his daughter."

"Oh." Claire's breath caught in her throat as the truth of that statement sank in. Looking again at the man who sat before her, she spotted Frankie's features. The texture of the hair, the high forehead, the shape of the jaw. But what did it mean?

"What do you want with her?" Tamiel voiced Claire's question.

"Nothing. Just to be her father," Yakum said softly. "To guide her through this tough time while she figures out exactly who she is. Like I do with all my children." He slumped in his chair, the fire in his eyes dimming with his words. "Not human. Not angel. She's confused; she believes that she has no control over her own future. So she's acting out."

This was the man who, according to Tamiel, wanted to create a demonic army?

He waved a hand in the direction of the hearth. "Look." Blue flames shot up, and, like a movie, images of Frankie as a younger girl rolled in the fire. Claire recognized the room. Frankie stood in this very chamber. Her face hard and tense, her hands clenched tight. There was no sound, but Claire could read Frankie's lips. She was saying, "It's not fair," over and over. Yakum stood by her side. His posture was relaxed, and his hands were open and accepting. Frankie backed away from him as she railed at the world.

"See," Yakum said, looking at Claire, "she's not content with being stronger and faster than the average human. She wants what you have, godmother. Access to the magic."

In the fire, the view of Frankie shifted to a close-up. She pounded a fist in the air while tears rolled down her cheeks. Claire couldn't read everything she was saying, but there was definitely a bunch of "fucking" and "fuck" and one or two "shitheads."

"So you expect us to believe that this is all just about a teenager throwing a tantrum." Tamiel slashed her sword into the fire, sending a ripple through the images. "What about you sending the demons after her?"

"They were just programmed to get her and bring her home. Thank you very much for stopping that." Sarcasm dripped in his tone. "I've personally tried a bunch of times to fetch her. She won't come with me. And now, thanks to you, I'm out of options."

Tamiel had the grace to look slightly contrite.

Yakum lowered his hand; the flame in the hearth dipped and the images faded away. "What did you think it was about? That someone down here had gone round the bend?"

Tamiel didn't answer.

"You and I are on the same side."

Tamiel shook her head. "I don't think so."

"I don't know what lies our brethren are telling you up there. I mean when they actually bother to talk to each other. But the only thing that makes me a fallen angel is that I've chosen my own path. Sure, I've done a few things that maybe aren't in the canon—"

"Like raping Abal?"

Yakum sighed deeply. "They tell the story all wrong. I assume you've heard their version?"

Tamiel nodded curtly and didn't mention she had been one of the ones spreading it. Claire's gaze darted back to Yakum. Much to her surprise, she had completely relaxed into this exchange. She couldn't wait to see what was going to happen next.

"Then I guess the truth would surprise you. Abal was one of the greatest loves of my life. She begged me to take her away. Her uncle and her cousin were maybe two nights away from defiling her. Them, not me. One day, she saw me helping a man in the marketplace with a little spell that doubled the potency of his herbs and spices. She implored me to help her."

"For God's sake, you should have said no."

The flame in Yakum's eyes flared. "I couldn't. She was in terrible trouble. You would have done the same."

"Not if I wasn't assigned to her. And I certainly wouldn't have gone any further."

"My only sin was that I was lonely."

He raised his hand, and the blaze jumped in the hearth. Images of Yakum with a beautiful, raven-haired woman, dancing in another room from another time, filled the flames.

"It would be easy to manipulate the fire."

"True. But I'm not. Did you ever think to question the choir when they spoke of my guilt?"

Again, Tamiel said nothing.

Claire's heart went out to her. The conversation, well, really the implications, were well outside her wheelhouse, but clearly Tamiel had as many prejudices about Yakum as Claire had had about Tamiel in the beginning. It was the same everywhere. Believing the worst about someone else allowed you to believe the best about yourself.

"Tamiel," Yakum said softly, "are you really telling me that you've never considered dallying with your charges?"

A deeper flush swept across Tamiel's cheeks.

"Ah, maybe even right now?"

What did that mean? Claire tilted her head. Did Tamiel have a thing for Frankie, or someone else?

"Yakum," Tamiel said, her voice deep with emotion, "leave it."

"Okay, okay. But there has to be balance in the world, and sometimes to achieve that, you need to walk your own path. Take my advice."

"That will be the day."

"Fine. Then just help me with Francesca. You'll realize I'm right eventually."

"Speaking of help, how did she get onto the client list at the FGC?" Claire asked. Despite everything, she was beginning to believe him.

He turned to her. "The FGC didn't generate her case. But I think you already know that."

Claire nodded.

"When I was explaining the greater scope of the world we live in, I told her about the FGC. It took her almost two years, and even now I don't really know how she did it. Kids these days can hack into any system. Basically, she created an open file and sent it to your boss."

"And you didn't think to tell us?" Tamiel asked.

"Would you have believed me?" To Claire he said, "You really should get a much more secure system."

"Why on earth would she want to be a client of the FGC?" Claire asked, spinning the conversation in the only direction that mattered right now.

"To get one of those." He pointed to Claire's hand.

"A wand?"

"She wants a way to access her connection to the magic. She feels it is her birthright, and maybe it is, but I kept telling her she can't steal it. She has to earn it with the right choices."

Claire tilted her head. Could he be right? Frankie had tried to grab Carothann in the alley. Her touch had caused its filter to break. In her room, hadn't she admitted she was hunting for it after the battle? Hadn't she also commented on Juliette's wand, Baltine, almost as soon as they met?

How could she have missed all the signs? Was she so pushed into one interpretation of the world around her that she had forgotten other possibilities could exist? She glanced down at Carothann. Frankie's band still ran around the bottom of the slender branch, but now it was more black than maroon.

"You know what I say is true, don't you, godmother?"

Claire pursed her lips and nodded.

"Seriously?" Tamiel asked.

Claire reached out and pulled her across the room. Taut muscle ran beneath her clothes. Tamiel's arm felt solid and comforting in her hand.

She showed her wand and tapped the black band. "Carothann is changing. Becoming something more. It knows somehow. Look, I'm not endorsing what he does. But he seems—and I can't believe I'm saying this—reasonable. We've only known Frankie for a day. I don't know. She could be playing us."

"So could he."

"True." Claire glanced up. Tamiel's gaze was completely focused on her. In any other situation, it would be intoxicating. "Can I be honest with you?"

"Always." Tamiel touched her arm.

"Before meeting you in the alley, my life played out in black and white. The GA was our enemy, and only I was on

the side of right. Now we're working together, and Yakum…"
She paused while she searched for the right words. "Do you
think maybe that you're with him where I was with you a few
days ago?"

"You mean prejudiced."

"I mean inexperienced…" Claire raised her eyebrows "…
but wise enough to know when you could be wrong." She gave
Tamiel a moment to ponder her words. "He absolutely could
be lying about Frankie, but he did get one thing right. Nothing
is all good or bad, and we can't buy into this black-or-white
understanding of the world. We need to make our own choices
of how to move forward and not let some antiquated system
like the FGC or even the GA tell us what to do."

The fire danced in Tamiel's irises as she seemed to consider
what Claire had said. Claire could see the conflict raging in
their depths. Whoever had said the eyes were the windows to
the soul must have been looking at an angel when they said it.

"You think we should give him a chance to at least prove
himself wrong?" Tamiel asked.

"At least."

"She makes a good point, if I do say so myself." Yakum rose
from the throne.

Tamiel swung back to him. "That was a private conversation."

"Yes, but it was about me," he said as if that were enough
explanation. "So, Tamiel, are you in with the godmother and
me, or are you out?"

With the decision upon her now, Tamiel froze. Claire bit
her bottom lip. She didn't have an exigency plan if—

"I'm in." She met Claire's gaze.

Her shoulders dropped, and relief whipped through her as
she stared back.

Yakum walked over to the far wall and tapped a red stone twice with his knuckle. A hidden door swung open, revealing a cache of weapons both human and magical. He reached in past several swords to pull out a thin iron ring about the size of a small bowl. He tossed it up in the air and caught it. "Excellent. Let's go get my daughter."

Yakum wasn't the only one desperate for a meeting. As soon as the three of them slipped back into the museum, Claire contacted Juliette. Carothann bristled at the request, but Claire pushed the thought hard at the wand until she heard Juliette's voice reach out from its tip.

"Son of a banshee, Claire. Get back here. This girl is... I really need you to run point on this one."

"Sure, sure, Juliette. I'll take over, but let's meet to discuss it. Not at the office. How about...in Frankie's alley? I'll send you the coordinates."

"Why?"

"It's complicated."

"Just come back." The wand vibrated with Juliette's irritation. "Seriously, that girl needs a lot of attention, and she keeps bumping into me all the time as if she's looking for something. It's weird. I just don't—"

"I'll explain when I see you, but believe me, you don't want to have this meeting at the office. Oh, and keep your wand away from her."

A boy with freckles rushed over and tried to touch Carothann's shining tip. "Oh cool. Is that some kind of new app? How does it work?"

"Who is that?" Juliette asked.

"Nobody." Claire jerked the wand away from the boy. "I'll explain everything when I see you."

Yakum spun the child toward the exit. "Yes. It's a new app, and the wand part is in the gift store. They're selling fast. Chop-chop."

"Oh my God. Thanks. I totally want one!" The boy darted off.

"See, you need me." Yakum tilted his head in mild challenge.

"You are not our friend," Tamiel said.

"But I'm not your enemy either." He slid a hand under each of their elbows and steered them into the next room. "We better get moving before that human comes back."

The big purple letters over the door spelled *Movie & TV Props*, and the room itself was jammed with famous objects pulled right off current studios and sets. There, right in the middle, was a big blue telephone booth. *Police Public Call Box* was written on top. Yakum pulled open the door and herded them in while no one was looking.

"It really is bigger on the inside," he said with a grin on his face.

"Sorry?" Claire glanced at Tamiel. She was glaring at Yakum, her normally lovely features screwed up in annoyance.

"Human TV. You really should make some time. It's quite good." He moved over to a futuristic console in the center of the box. "I can make you a list."

"It would be faster if we just all met there," Tamiel said.

"But not as much fun." Yakum yanked down a lever, and the noise of a car key scraping across a piano wire filled the air. "Because this prop is real! Well, a real teleporter. Not a time machine. That would be ridiculous."

"Oh for goodness's sake. This isn't a game." Tamiel pulled the door open to reveal the alley from downtown. "You first, Claire."

The alley was different than Claire remembered. At this time of day, it was completely empty. The other thing that had changed was Frankie's art. In the twenty-four hours since they had been here, someone had graffitied the graffiti. Angry black slashes tarnished the blue and gold swirls. What had sung out as a message of encouragement now rang with bleakness and despair. Claire shivered. Was it an omen?

She sent the coordinates to Juliette's wand, Carothann jumping into action this time almost before she had sent the thought. She liked this new version of her wand more and more.

Only moments later, a shimmer in the middle of the alley announced the arrival of Juliette and Frankie. Juliette came as her true self. The change, however, was in Frankie. Gone was the timid girl. Frankie stood tall and strong, and if Claire wasn't mistaken, even a hint of fire danced in her eyes.

As soon as Juliette saw the trio, the color drained from her face. "What the—? Claire, are you crazy?" She squeezed her eyes shut and at the same time flung a hand out to cover Frankie's.

The girl stepped easily out of Juliette's reach and leveled a harsh look at Yakum. "Hello, Father." Gone, too, was her teenage whine. She spit the last word out as if it were poison.

"Hello, Francesca," Yakum said. "You've been busy, I see."

"With no help from you."

"You didn't want the kind of help I was willing to give and the kind you actually needed."

Juliette opened her eyes but used her hands as blinders. She stared only at Claire. "Will someone please tell me what is going on here?"

"I think we've all been played by our client," Claire said. "Frankie, do you want to answer Juliette's question?"

"I sure do. It's so not fair. I got powers, and I can't use them. You got wands, and you're idiots—"

"Excuse me?" Juliette shifted her glare to Frankie.

Frankie let out an exasperated sigh. "Man, you're just like my stupid stepmom. You don't notice anything unless it's about yourself. Can't you all see? I just want a chance to become what I was always meant to be."

"Which is?" Tamiel asked.

"I don't know. But he's trying to control everything I do. I just want a little freedom."

"Please, daughter," Yakum said quietly. "Come back with me and we'll try to work this out together."

Claire glanced at Yakum. He stood relaxed, shoulders down, his face a mask of patience. Her heart went out to him. Fallen angel or not, he clearly loved his daughter, and Claire knew how hard it was to mother, or at least godmother, a teenager who thought she knew best.

"What do you say?" Yakum raised his hands. "Can we try this again?"

"You've got to be kidding me. I'd rather stay with that asshat..." She waved a finger at Juliette "...than go with you."

Juliette rolled back on her heels, striking a defensive posture. She shook Baltine at Frankie like a schoolmarm fussing at her students.

"Besides, I don't need any of you anymore." Frankie twirled quickly, showing some of that inherited angel speed, and plucked Juliette's wand right out of her fingers.

Juliette's mouth dropped open to form a perfectly round O. Her body froze as her gaze darted around, clearly trying to make sense of what had just happened.

"No!" Claire cried and jumped for the wand.

At the same time, Frankie backpedaled down the alley, her prize clutched in her hand.

Baltine bucked in Frankie's fingers; golden shards of magic shot out of its tip in protest and cut across the alley. One sliced into Claire's face, and warm blood trickled down her cheek.

"Drop it, Frankie," Claire shouted. "You can't handle it."

"Yes, I can." Her face, though, had already reddened with the effort. Frankie clutched the wand with both hands, trying to ride out the convulsions, which were multiplying by the moment. "It will accept my thoughts. I just have to break the filter in this one too." Her brows furrowed as she glared at the wand.

"Don't!" Juliette edged away from the group. "The filter is what keeps us safe."

"You knew?" Claire whipped around to face her boss.

"Of course. We can't let you loose in the field with unlimited power."

There it was: the FGC philosophy laid out neatly in the juxtaposition between *we* and *you* in that sentence. No matter how this played out, Claire could never accept that betrayal.

Right now, though, Frankie was in trouble. A crack resonated through the alley, just like when Frankie had grabbed Carothann two days earlier. The filter, Claire guessed, had snapped in Baltine.

"I did it!" she cried. "Harder than your wand when—"

WOOSH. Energy zoomed into the alley and rushed into the wand. Frankie's whole body contorted as though she was in a seizure. Golden bursts of magic exploded from the top of her head and from the tips of her feet. Magic in full force was coursing through her. Claire knew from recent experience that she and Baltine could only hang on for so long.

Yakum waved a hand, but whatever magic he threw at Frankie was ineffective. It ricocheted and knocked him squarely to the ground. "Help her." Yakum's voice cracked. "Please."

Throw. The voice was in Claire's head.

"What, Tamiel?" If she were going to give her instructions, she could at least make them clear.

"Not me," the angel said breathlessly.

Then who? Not Yakum. He was staring only at Frankie. Spheres of pulsating energy began to grow around her.

Juliette gasped as she must have realized they were all in danger. She slunk down the alley and disappeared around the corner.

"For Chimera's sake, drop the wand, Frankie," Claire shouted.

Carothann bucked in her hand. *Throw.* It wasn't a voice as much as an image.

It was the wand, not Tamiel, who was telling her what to do. Carothann was actually communicating with her!

She had no time to stand around and wonder at this new, miraculous development. The energy surrounding Frankie buckled and began to expand toward them in a torrent of power.

THROW. The image reared up larger in Claire's head. Surely she wasn't just supposed to toss a conduit to pure magic straight into an ever-expanding energy field. It seemed like the worst idea imaginable. But she trusted Carothann with her life. She held the wand high. Purpose coursed through its wood. She heaved, and the wand soared across the alley toward the expansion of energy.

Carothann tumbled end over end and flew into the mass of power hurling toward them. It wasn't going to make it in time; the bristling wave was almost on them. Claire reached over to grab Tamiel's outstretched arm. If this was the end, Tamiel was the last thing she wanted to feel. She waited for the impact.

It didn't come.

Carothann had arrived at the center of the energy and hovered over Frankie. It lit up brighter than Claire had ever seen it. Another deafening crack filled the air. Baltine broke at its center and disintegrated in a flash of light. Frankie screamed, her hands blistering from the intensity. Suddenly the expanding, destructive force fell back, imploding as it went. It continually folded in on itself, rushing into Carothann with unnatural speed.

And then it was over. Frankie fell to the ground, out cold. Carothann clattered to the pavement a few feet away.

Yakum rushed to his daughter and pressed his palms to her shoulders. A heat wave Claire could feel all the way across the alley dove into Frankie. Instantly, Tamiel was by his side. "Can I help?"

Yakum grabbed her hands and directed them to Frankie's hips. Soon the girl's whole body was bathed in the visible healing energy of the angels.

Claire walked slowly past them to Carothann. From a distance, it looked fine, and she carried that slim hope with her for the last few steps. But when she stood over it, she saw the crack running from tip to tail. She picked it up and stared, almost without comprehension, at the broken wand in her hand. There was magic still in its core, but it was fading fast. A cold numbness pierced her stomach. She sent positive thoughts directly at it. *Heal. Be well.*

Nothing changed.

How long she stood like that, looking at her wand, she didn't know. A comforting hand finally dropped on her shoulder and squeezed. A small jolt of energy shot through her body. It must have been healing energy because instantly Claire's nerves weren't quite as ragged and she was able to take a breath that actually filled her lungs. She met Tamiel's gaze.

"Can you fix it?" Tamiel asked.

"No." Claire held the wand out to her. "Can you?"

Tamiel ran a hand across the wand. It lit up for an instant with the angel's healing energy, but as soon as Tamiel withdrew her hand, it looked even more brittle.

"No. I can't. I'm so sorry. I guess it doesn't work that way."

They both looked at the wand. "It saved Frankie," Tamiel said finally.

Claire glanced down the alley. Frankie sat with her back to a brick wall. She looked dazed, but she would live.

"It saved us all. Carothann sacrificed itself for all of us," Tamiel said and squeezed her shoulder again.

Claire's mind cleared. True. Carothann's actions were beyond noble. It had put the well-being of a client ahead of its own welfare. She was so selfish to be thinking about herself right now.

But—and it was such a big but—what would life be like without Carothann? The golden glow that always shimmered from within her wand was starting to die. Frankie's band faded altogether, and Abby's went from bright green to a sickly color like pond scum.

She knew what she had to do. She didn't have much time.

"Tamiel? I need one last favor."

Claire practically flew up the broken stairs to the second floor of Abby's apartment building. Tamiel had sent her over in a flash. The angel's unfamiliar magic still swirled around her, squeezing her in odd places like a sweater that was too tight. She prayed Abby was home. Carothann had one last flick, maybe two, and she couldn't waste it on chasing Abby around.

The door to two-ten was ajar, and a pop song in perfect pitch drifted outside. Abby actually sounded…happy.

Yes, she knew exactly what she had to do. She looked down at Carothann in her hand. *Do you have one more in you? Please hang on.* She slipped inside.

Abby had her back to the door and something frying in a pan on the stove.

"Abby," Claire said softly.

Abby turned, flinging what turned out to be a grilled cheese sandwich onto the floor. "Finally. Where have you been? I read your version of Cinderella. I know how it works. I'm ready."

Claire choked out a sad laugh. "Abby, I've been thinking. We've been going about this all wrong. Actually, I've been going about everything wrong. Your happily ever after isn't a man. It's…." Claire faltered and glanced down at Carothann. As raw as she was, she couldn't give a long explanation. "Look, get your phone. It's easier if I just show you."

Abby stepped over the grilled cheese and grabbed the new iPhone off the coffee table. "You're not going to take it back, are you?"

"Get ready." Claire sighed. "You're about to have the most important phone call of your life. You might even want to put the spatula down."

She raised Carothann and pointed it at the phone. She could feel the wand pulling hard at the little magic it could still access.

Please. An image of hope flooded her head. The wand wanted one last moment as much as she did. It wouldn't be easy. There were all sorts of paperwork and releases, memories to implant, MP3 files of Abby's voice to create and send to the right people. *You can do it.* She sent the thought to Carothann, and the wand trembled in her hand. She flicked it at the phone. Did it have the strength?

The phone buzzed. Claire squeezed the wand in a gentle thank-you. "You better answer it."

"Hello," Abby said.

"Hello. Abby Rodgers?" a thin, male voice came from the speaker.

"Yes."

"This is Russ from *The Song.*"

Abby put her hand over the phone as her eyes widened. "The TV show? For real?"

"For real," Claire said.

"I don't know why," Russ continued, "it's been so hard to get in touch with you, but look. There's a car coming to your address in Hollywood in five minutes to take you to the studio."

"What for?" Abby said, her voice also thin with amazement.

"For your rehearsal with the studio band, and our producer wants you to go on camera to tell everyone what it will mean to you if you're chosen by one of our coaches. What song are you singing again?"

Abby looked to Claire, who whispered. "The one you were just singing. It's wonderful."

"'It Must Be Magic.'"

"I like that song." Russ's voice drifted out of the phone. "And I shouldn't tell you this, but that's a particular favorite of June Jones. I've seen your audition tape. You could go far on this show." He hung up with a click.

"Am I really going to be on *The Song*?"

"You're going to have to be chosen, but with a voice like that... You heard him. You'll do well. I truly think it's your destiny. But you need to grab it. No one is going to hand it to you. Not even me." She could feel Carothann fading in her hand. It wouldn't be long now. "Oh, and Abby?"

"Yes?"

Claire waved her wand for the last time. "Be grateful." It wasn't much, a little birth blessing twenty-two years late, but it was all Carothann had left. And Claire hoped it might make all the difference to Abby.

As the last of Carothann's magic reached out to caress the girl, the hardness in her eyes softened. The first true smile, at least the first Claire had seen, jumped to her lips.

"Thank you," Abby said as if she truly meant it. "Singing has always been my dream."

"Then go get it. I'll lock up."

Abby walked out the door with a new lightness in her step. Claire looked down again at Carothann. It had slipped away during that last exchange. And now, just a second later, Claire held only a small branch, dry and dull, in her hand.

Good-bye, old friend. The emptiness in her stomach and chest spread everywhere. Head down, Claire trudged to the door and froze.

With Carothann gone, she had no idea how to get home.

Claire didn't know when she had last been so tired. Getting to Santa Monica from Hollywood without magic had been exhausting. She had tried calling Tamiel while she was still at Abby's. In her head. Out loud. Nothing. In the end, she had grabbed a fistful of quarters from a paper cup marked with

LAUNDRY in red Sharpie. Three buses and a half a mile walk, and she was finally home.

Was this what life would be like from now on? The worst part was that she had way too much time to think. On the first bus, all the way down Sunset Boulevard, she'd just stared out the window at the huge mansions. Too numb to cry. But when she'd transferred to the Big Blue Bus Line, problems with no solutions began to circle in her head. She couldn't go back to the FGC. Juliette, the coward, was probably there right now, spinning a story where Claire had made a million missteps, and she, Juliette, had tried to stop her. No matter what the future brought, she would never work with Juliette again.

Besides, even if the FGC did take her back into another department and city, thanks to her poor cousin and those fairy pictures, she already knew what happened when a mistake, or even the perception of an error, followed you around. On top of that were the filters in the wands. How had Tamiel put it? Those filters had cut operatives off at the knees. Another betrayal she just couldn't get beyond.

She closed her eyes and shook her head. In her mind's eye, she imagined her name on Juliette's case board darkening from gold to black. It was that simple. She had left the FGC. Just like Pierre. It was the stupidest…and the bravest thing she had ever done.

What on earth would she do next?

She wouldn't think about it now. Instead, she would sleep until she woke up and then decide what she wanted for breakfast and then lunch and finally dinner. Maybe she would head over to the farmers' market on Arizona Avenue to see what stone fruit was ripest. She could take it slow. There would be centuries to figure out how to navigate this new future as a godmother without magic.

When she got home, her tiny living room seemed hugely empty. The couch and the coffee table took up most of the room, but what wasn't there loomed larger.

"Tamiel?" she said and hoped against hope the angel would walk into existence by the coffee table or from the kitchen doorway.

Again nothing.

She sniffed at the air. Salt and brine from the ocean breeze tickled her nose, but no pine, no fresh mountain air.

Okay, I can deal with this. Why had she even thought Tamiel might be here? The case was closed. Frankie was back where she belonged, and there was no reason anymore for Tamiel to come calling.

She squared her shoulders and headed over to her tiny office in a nook of the room. Carothann's box sat on the edge of her desk like always. She ran a finger across its top, and even though a tightness squeezed her chest, she finally flipped it open. She couldn't catch her breath. The velvet-lined case resembled a casket more than a refuge, and sealing Carothann up inside was the end of so much more than her wand. She closed her eyes and forced a breath deep into her lungs before gently tucking Carothann into the velvet folds. It looked so small and pale against the rich, red fabric. She couldn't bring herself to close the lid.

Tears sprang to her eyes as she turned away and stood in the middle of her living room, frozen, not knowing what to feel or where to go next.

Suddenly Tamiel stepped into the space right in front of her and without a word took Claire in her arms.

Claire pressed her forehead to the angel's shoulder. The silver cloth of Tamiel's shirt rose up along her shoulder, caressing Claire's head and repositioning it so her cheek rested along Tamiel's neck. The familiar mountain breeze fresh with pine rolled over her, and then a scent she had never smelled before. It brimmed with hints of jasmine, vanilla, and other things she couldn't identify. It smelled like…like…bliss.

Let the pain go. Tamiel's voice, gentle and calm, touched her mind. *Celebrate Carothann's choice. Mourn its loss, but honor its sacrifice.*

Tamiel slid a hand down her back. The embrace buzzed with healing energy, this time targeting her spirit rather than her body. The emptiness eased a little, and the clenching around her heart loosened. Claire didn't care that she was being manipulated. What if this connection was the *dangerous angel trick* the FGC claimed it was? So what. If someone had the talent to heal mind, body, and soul, shouldn't she use it?

Claire relaxed in Tamiel's arms and breathed deeply. The scent, the touch, the comforting voice in her head washed over her and drove her anxiety and grief into the background. The emotions were still there, but no longer overwhelming.

"Better?" Tamiel asked, pulling away.

Claire nodded. "Where were you?"

"With Yakum. He sends his regards." Tamiel tilted her head for a beat. "I think you were right about him. Frankie has a real shot at being okay, and not just physically."

"I thought that…" Claire's voice cracked. "I didn't know if I would see you again. I mean with Frankie's case being closed and all."

"I had to come back."

"Why?"

"Because," Tamiel shrugged, "I was never sent here for Frankie."

Claire's brows furrowed.

"I'm *your* guardian angel."

"What?" She had heard the words, but surely she had misunderstood.

"We're not just assigned humans, you know."

Son of a banshee. She should have known right from the start in the alley, when she'd almost fallen headlong into those flaming eyes. That was when Tamiel had claimed her. Or maybe when Tamiel kept sending her guidance and messages. She was a blooming idiot. She had been from that first moment in the alley until—

"And if I'm being truthful," Tamiel cut into her thoughts, "I had to come back for this too." She paused only for an instant before she moved.

Claire didn't know if it was another one of those kooky angel tricks, but everything swung into slow motion. As Tamiel leaned in closer, the fire in her eyes rose into incandescent points and the light spread across her face.

Claire was mesmerized and started to tip forward before she squeezed her own eyes shut to prevent herself from falling into Tamiel. Robbed of her sight, her other senses took over. New smells of sunshine and freshly cut grass enveloped her. As Tamiel's head came closer, the energy that always swirled around her reached out to Claire. It caressed her face, running across her brow and down her cheeks, circling close to her mouth. Eyes still closed, Claire swallowed hard, waiting for—

Tamiel's lips dropped on hers. The touch was so soft Claire was uncertain that their mouths had actually met. But then her lips started to tingle, and Tamiel's hand slid down her side to her hip. Tamiel pulled her closer, and the kiss deepened.

The fleeting thought of it being too soon after Carothann sailed over her, but no, she needed the closeness, the chance to forget for just a moment. Claire reached out too and tentatively circled her arms around Tamiel's waist. The silver material of her clothes pooled up around her hands, encouraging her to hold on more tightly. As if she needed any encouragement.

Tamiel's tongue played over Claire's lips, teasing them apart.

Claire moaned and slid her tongue forward. Her mouth was burning hot. The fire? Was it there too? The heat didn't burn. Instead, the tingling still on her lips shot straight to her core. Her whole body shook with desire. Could she handle this? She broke the kiss and opened her eyes.

Tamiel stood before her, longing etched into her face. Her lips trembled. Surely she wasn't nervous? She cupped Claire's cheek and ran her thumb over Claire's lips all the way to the corner and then let her hand drop.

"Claire, I would like to be with you tonight." She glanced down as though she was afraid. Of Claire's response? Or what this would mean for her personally?

"Me too," she whispered, not sure if this was the best time to leap. Her nerves were still so raw with the day's events, but not jumping was unthinkable.

She slid her hand into Tamiel's and started for the bedroom.

"Oh," Tamiel whispered, "we don't need a bed." She pulled her close, raised her hand, and kissed the knuckles. Then, slowly she lowered her mouth to Claire's in a tender kiss. Claire sensed she had just meant the gesture for reassurance and comfort, but Claire caught Tamiel's lower lip between her teeth and nibbled. Now it was Tamiel's turn to groan. She heard it in her ears and in her mind.

This was going to be very interesting. Just how interesting, she couldn't have possibly guessed.

Tamiel's arms came around her, hugging her tight, and Claire instinctively leaned into her. Good thing too, because her feet had left the ground. At first, she thought it was just another weird sensation, like smelling bliss, but when she glanced down, they were unbelievably at least four feet off the ground. Tamiel leaned back into the air, bringing Claire with her. At first, she fought the sensation. Her brain told her she would crash to the ground, but when she didn't, she gave in to the feeling of floating. It was exhilarating and terrifying all at once.

"Can I take this off?" Tamiel cut to the chase. She had her thumb under the strap of Claire's top.

"Yes," she answered in a husky voice she almost didn't recognize.

Tamiel snuck her hand under the strap and began pulling, taking the entire dress with her. In an instant Claire was naked. Magic or supreme skill? She didn't care or even think about the difference anymore when Tamiel caught her face between her hands and fused their lips together in a kiss that sent heat sizzling straight to her groin. Everything down there tightened up.

"Not fair," Claire murmured against Tamiel's mouth. "You've still got clothes on."

The silver fabric rustled and then completely disappeared. Neat trick. Claire ran a hand down the angel's body in fluttering circles. She was all long, lean muscle and smooth planes. Her skin was almost translucent, and her small breasts rose and fell with her ragged breaths. Claire reached over and took one in her hands. Tamiel arched up into the caress, her nipple hardening instantly. Desire rolled below Claire's belly, and she shuddered in pleasure at how Tamiel reacted to her touch. Too much, too soon. Claire had to slow down for both their sakes.

She rolled over onto her, wondering only for an instant if Tamiel could take her weight and still keep them aloft. She bent into Tamiel's neck and feathered kisses up along her cheek.

Her smell, whatever it was, was intoxicating. She nibbled up to Tamiel's ear before sucking the lobe into her mouth. And then she worked her way back down and ended back at the perfect breast. She circled around it, kissing, nibbling, even gently biting until she swept her tongue over the nipple, teasing until it was hard again.

Tamiel moaned and flung her hands out into the air as if to brace herself. Claire took as much of her as she could into her mouth; she couldn't get enough of this woman. Suddenly she was slipping off the breast. Tamiel had drifted up under Claire, and Claire's mouth was sliding down her stomach. Claire laid both palms flat against Tamiel's belly as she floated away. Her soft skin rolled over hard muscle, and Claire closed her eyes, trying to take in as much of the new sensation as possible.

Tamiel's motion halted just as Claire's hands and mouth reached the curls below her belly. Her warm, musty scent enveloped Claire, and she groaned, sure in the knowledge that Tamiel wanted this as much as she did.

Please? The question popped into her head almost without language. But longing ran deep in the thought.

"My pleasure."

There was no preamble. Tamiel floated up over Claire. When Claire had been on top, there was the pretense that gravity held them together, but now Claire drifted in the air as if she were an astronaut in space. The only place they were physically connected was where her mouth and hands still touched Tamiel's body. All her awareness of Tamiel was funneled into those three contact points. Nothing had ever been so erotic.

Tamiel drifted a bit further until Claire's mouth hovered right between her legs. Claire tipped her head back, and Tamiel rose up and over her mouth.

Claire dipped her tongue into the soft folds. She tasted like sunshine. Spread wide above her, Tamiel sent her sighs and moans straight into Claire's head. Claire had always liked the sounds of lovemaking. They turned her on. But hearing the noises inside her mind sent tiny pulses of heat deep to her core. She dove in with abandon. She stroked up one side of Tamiel and down the other, making wide circles around her swollen clit. When neither of them could take it anymore, she took Tamiel into her mouth and sucked.

Tamiel bucked above her and bent over to twist her hands into Claire's thick hair.

Claire held her close as waves of excitement rode through her body. When the release came, it surged in both their heads.

Claire still floated in the magic bubble. She flung out her arms, trying to swim up to Tamiel, but Tamiel was already on her way down. Their bodies slid against each other. The touch, not bound by gravity, was electric, and Claire's nerves tingled every place that skin met skin. Tamiel pulled Claire into her lap. She rested lightly in Tamiel's arms, almost hovering, and with no pressure points, she couldn't anticipate where Tamiel's hands or lips would caress her. The surprise sent shivers straight down her spine—Tamiel's lips on Claire's mouth, her hands on her breasts, her feather touches sliding down Claire's back. Tamiel was everywhere and nowhere. Claire closed her eyes to drink in the sensation. Desire ripped through her. One hand moved from her behind into the space between her legs.

Never had her body been so swollen and ready.

Tamiel played with her curls and then teased her open, running delicate strokes up and down her inner thighs. Claire's legs fell apart almost of their own accord, and Tamiel slid one finger into her soft folds. She brushed against her clit, sending spasms of delight radiating out in all directions.

You like that. Tamiel's voice was in her head. *Do you like this?*

Tamiel circled her clit with several fingers, never quite touching it, teasing Claire until she couldn't take it anymore.

"Please," Claire said.

Tamiel flicked her thumb across the nub. Claire sucked in a breath and tensed. All sensation flooded to right between her legs. Tamiel had a magic touch, no surprise there. A flame of pleasure ignited deep in Claire. As Tamiel stroked and pulled and caressed, it blossomed, rising higher and faster.

Tamiel must have sensed she was close, because her other hand hovered lower and slowly slid inside with one finger, then two. Claire moaned and arched into the touch as Tamiel eased forward until she was deep within Claire.

She froze, letting her fingers spread as far as Claire could take.

Claire gasped at the unbelievable sense of fullness.

More?

"Yes." Her answer was no more than a breath.

Tamiel began to move in earnest. She caressed Claire with her hands while nibbling and licking Claire's neck.

You're so beautiful. Tamiel's voice was inside her head, urging her on.

Tension and heat rose below her belly, threatening to take Claire over completely. She arched in Tamiel's lap. Magic rushed in and kept her comfortably aloft. All she had to do was relax into the tension, reach for the release. Tamiel circled her fingers inside and found that sweet spot. Brightness exploded inside Claire, so intense that her body spasmed and shook. The magic held her rigid and taut so the waves of her orgasm crashed inside her like a tidal wave. There was no ebb. The sensation rose and rose.

"Tamiel," she cried out as she came apart.

The next morning, they lay cuddled together in Claire's bed. Lying down on a mattress felt so pedestrian now that Claire knew what was possible. But Tamiel had wrapped her arms around her all night long, and Claire reveled in her touch. Never had she been closer to anyone.

"You awake?" Tamiel asked. Her voice was magical.

"Yes." Claire snuggled into Tamiel's embrace. "Did you stay like this all night? Awake? Holding me?"

"I did. You were in pain and you're my charge. Where else would I go?"

She closed her eyes and concentrated on Tamiel's strong arms around her. Suddenly, a terrible thought hit Claire. "You didn't…? Last night wasn't…?" What if the best sex she'd ever had was just part of the GA service?

"God, no. I've never wanted anything so much," Tamiel said, almost as if she had read her mind. She probably had.

"Me neither." Heat rose to Claire's cheeks. But she liked the way Tamiel called it exactly the way it was.

"We're not supposed to consort with clients. Ever. But you're different. Not a client really. More like a colleague."

Was she really? Was Tamiel lying to Claire and herself? That conundrum was something they would have to sort out later. Right now Claire was starving. She untangled from Tamiel, got out of bed, and froze.

The angel lying naked on her bed was one of the most breathtaking things she had ever seen. Had the great artists of the world had angels of their own as models? No other explanation was possible.

"Oh, sorry." Tamiel shrugged her silver clothes back into existence. They flowed over her like a babbling brook until she was fully clothed. "I don't know what the conventions are after…something so wonderful."

Adorable.

"Apparently, neither do I." Claire chuckled and reached for Carothann at her hip to flick her own dress on.

The room began to spin.

It wasn't in her magic pocket and would never be again.

Tamiel jumped from the bed and rushed to her side. "Let me help."

Claire's favorite green dress settled on her. Her hair tied itself up into a neat bun. But it was no good. Sadness crashed in on her from the inside. She rushed from the room.

She averted her eyes from the desk as she walked to the kitchen. The box's lid was still up, and she couldn't take even a glimpse of the dead wand lying inside.

A minute later, she stood in front of the fridge, door open, looking at Greek yogurt, OJ, and some seeded sourdough bread. She had woken up so hungry, and now nothing on the shelves tempted her.

Tamiel appeared at the kitchen door, her brows wrinkled. "You okay?"

"I forgot it was gone. How could I forget?" Grief and guilt washed over her.

Tamiel stepped over, her hand raised. "Let me help."

"No." Claire twisted away from her touch. The healing energy was tempting, to say the least, maybe even addictive. But that was why she had forgotten about Carothann in the first place. She needed to feel its loss. To let Tamiel soothe it away again with a shoulder rub or gentle caress almost defeated Carothann's sacrifice.

She shut the fridge—she wasn't hungry anymore—and met the angel's gaze head-on. The fire inside Tamiel's eyes flickered.

Claire took a step back. What the hell was she thinking? That after last night, she and Tamiel would become girlfriends? That she would ride off into the sunset with a guardian angel on her shoulder?

Could they even make it as a couple? She didn't even know how to live with *herself* without magic, without her job—let alone anyone else. A chill ran down her spine. How on earth was she supposed to start that conversation? She met Tamiel's gaze once again. Angel and godmother. They stood only a few feet and yet worlds apart.

Something unseen poked her in her side.

"Please, Tamiel. Don't." Claire closed her eyes and sighed.

"Don't what?"

"Whatever that is you're doing to my side. Stop poking me."

"That's not me." She shook her head with a quick motion.

Claire froze. Was she imaging things? No, there it was again. A sharp poke just below her rib cage.

Oh my! She recognized that touch!

She raced out to the living room and over to her desk. She grabbed Carothann's box and pulled it to her. Her wand must be alive. She would look down and see...

Pain stabbed the back of her throat.

...the same dead wood, the same crack all the way down its length.

What the hell was going on?

"What is it?" Tamiel echoed the question. She had moved to the living room door but hadn't crossed its threshold.

"I don't know?" Claire spun around the room. "I thought Carothann was calling, but it must be something else."

"Another wand?"

"Maybe."

"Does that happen?"

"Not normally, unless you're at the FGC. There's the place in Paris I told you about. Usually, you only feel the call if you're there."

"What about the wands in the wild?"

There was that. Could those rumors be true? But what had she done that was so deserving? Choosing her own path? It couldn't be that simple, could it?

The poking shifted to a tugging. Magic pulled at the hem of her dress as if it was inviting her on a quest.

"Whatever it is, it wants me to follow it."

"Are you going to?"

Claire threw up her hands as a response. This was uncharted territory, and it was way too soon to embrace another wand. But in her heart, she knew she would answer the call. A life without magic wasn't one she really wanted to figure out, and while this magic wasn't the steady, comforting flow of Carothann, it was magic and it was powerful.

"Yes," she said, admitting out loud what she already knew. She headed to the door.

Tamiel stood still in the doorframe to the kitchen. "May I come?"

Claire had her hand on the knob, her back to the door. Did she want Tamiel to join her? The first meeting with a wand was an intensely personal event.

Her gut reaction surprised her. Yes. She wanted Tamiel to come. That little hiccup in the kitchen had been more about her and her guilt over forgetting Carothann than about Tamiel. She would grieve and honor the wand whether they were together or not.

Besides, did they have to define this? Whatever this was. They weren't girlfriends—that was for humans. At that moment, she knew two things. She had to chase the magic, and she wanted Tamiel by her side while she did it. The rest of the future could sort itself out.

"Please," Claire said, turning around and reaching out a hand.

Tamiel smiled and bounded over like a puppy.

Sweet. Claire's heart melted. Again, with anyone else the exuberance would have been too much, but the emotions were so clearly new for Tamiel that Claire couldn't help getting swept up in them.

Tamiel slid her hand into Claire's and leaned in until their faces were almost touching. She whispered in Claire's ear, "Can I tell you something?"

"Yes."

"I've never been so invested in a case."

Claire chuckled and rested her temple against Tamiel's. They stood, not moving, for a beat. Strange, after their wonderful adventure last night, this touch was almost more intimate.

"Neither have I," Claire whispered back.

CHAPTER 5

Present

"It's so strong. I don't think I can control it." Claire trembled and stooped to rub her shin.

An older woman walking by with her terrier threw Claire a suspicious glance. Tamiel had glamoured at her approach, and for all intents and purposes, Claire was standing outside the sex toy store all alone, muttering about control. The woman pulled at the leash and hurried down the street.

Do you have to? Isn't it a partnership? Tamiel asked, just a voice in Claire's head. There was a comfort to it now.

"Yes, but Carothann felt like an old friend from the first time it called to me at the FGC. This feels more like a sparring partner."

A step up, then, Tamiel sent the thought.

Was it? A step up? The wand yanked at her. Exasperation, annoyance, and power. It was all there in the magic. Where the hell had it come from? Somewhere beyond the FGC clearly. Its appearance seemed way too easy and too quick. But Claire had transformed swiftly as well, not in person, but in attitude. In three days, her mind had opened up, and her reality had spread wide. Fast, yes. Too fast? Perhaps not.

Claire tamped down the fluttering in her chest and gave Tamiel a curt nod. Several deep breaths later she was at the frosted door, pulling it open to reveal the inside of the O.M.G-Spot.

Claire didn't know what to expect—she had never been in a shop like this—but it wasn't the clean lines and open feel that greeted her. Warm, white lights flooded down onto an oak floor that ran the length of the store. A nearby wall highlighted books and CDs while a table right in front of Claire advertised free lube with every hundred-dollar purchase. A perky woman with shoulder-length hair and glasses stood up behind the counter and eyed Claire as soon as she stepped inside.

"Fairy Godmother, are you looking for a wand?"

Claire flinched. How on earth could she possibly know?

"No, don't be embarrassed. Lots of our customers enjoy role play. I absolutely love that you wore your outfit in here. Such a classic choice."

Claire glanced down at the old-school green dress she always wore when she was her true self. Oh yeah. She hadn't bothered to change after Tamiel had dressed her. She never wore this outfit around humans who were not her clients.

"Looking for that wand to complete it?" the perky woman asked. "Here, let me show you our costume section."

Claire smiled thinly at the woman and pointed to a section in the back. She didn't know where she was headed, but the magic was dragging her forward as if she were caught in a tractor beam.

"Oh, right. Dildos and vibrators. Holler if you need any help."

Claire scooted by her and the display of edible underwear to a series of shelves that ran along the back wall.

Dildos of every imaginable shape and size sat clustered in themes. Silicone, strap-ons, and the famous G-spot model the store was named after.

She reached out to touch the sample of the Feel-So-Real and pulled back her fingers at the last moment.

"It's here?" Tamiel asked, shimmering into existence.

Claire nodded. The magic swirled around her like a gale-force wind. It was unlike anything she was familiar with, but already in the short time she had been exposed, this new magic was attacking all the wounds of the last few days and the ennui of decades. Tamiel's healing energy was fantastic, but more like a Band-Aid. This magic was like a life force. She did feel disloyal to Carothann, but already she was caught up in new possibilities and a new future.

She pushed aside the boxes and packages to find what she was looking for.

Whomping Willy—8 Inches of the Best Sex Toy Ever sat at the back of the shelf. That was where all the power was coming from.

"Seriously?" Tamiel chuckled.

"I'm afraid so." She reached out, and even before she grabbed it, the magic embraced her. "Hello, Willy," she said.

The image—no, just the idea—of a hug popped into her mind. Willy was communicating! She tingled all over. This is what magic should feel like. Not like the filtered kind the FGC gave them "for their own protection."

She broke into the packaging, praying the wand was inside and not the toy itself. She would feel absolutely ridiculous pulling out Whomping Willy every time she helped someone. But she would if she had to. The magic was just that good.

"Um." The shop woman darted over. "You're going to have to buy that first."

Tamiel immediately slid over to her and ran a hand down her arm. "In a minute."

The woman headed back to the counter without comment.

"Holy Harpy," Claire said. "Why do they have to make this so hard to open?"

Willy pushed from the inside, impatient.

"Here, let me." Tamiel waved a hand and the packaging fell to the floor, leaving all eight inches of Willy in Claire's hand. The idea of happiness flooded her mind. Willy was free. It was speaking to her, not in feelings or language, but something much more primitive than that. Something that didn't need to be interpreted or felt. It just was.

Claire ran the fingers of her free hand up and down the toy. Tamiel snorted softly.

"Don't go there." But Claire was chuckling herself.

"How can I not?"

"I'm looking for the wand. I can't find it. Holy Succubus, I think this is the wand." She flicked the dildo, and a golden stream came out of its tip. "That's just so wrong."

How on earth was she supposed to pull this out in the middle of a birth blessing? The parents would think she was a pervert.

"What's that thing down there?" Tamiel pointed to the ridge in the base of the toy.

"Oooh, thank goodness." Claire pushed, and a thin bamboo wand popped out of the flat bottom. The sex toy, not a velvet-lined box, was the wand's refuge. Welcome to the twenty-first century.

The wand was lovely. Light, strong, and aesthetically pleasing, with concentric rings of growth running up its stem. Not surprisingly, the wand fit her hand perfectly. Already, she felt as if she had known it for ages.

She flicked and a golden shower of magic flooded out of its tip. No filter, no barriers, no FGC. This was magic straight from the source. They would have to get used to each other, but they had centuries to do that. And she could design a new job, without Upper Administration or forms or deadlines. She could take her time and uncover what was truly right for her clients. She could work for herself...or even get a partner.

She spun to face Tamiel. The desire to share the moment with her told Claire all she needed to know about their relationship—or whatever it was. Tamiel grinned back, the smile softening the contours of her face. The fire in her eyes blossomed with happiness and if Claire wasn't crazy...love.

Joyous singing filled her head, but for the life of her, she couldn't tell if it was coming from the angel or the wand.

Did it even matter?

Willy snuggled into her hand at the same moment she stepped into Tamiel's embrace. Who knew what the future would bring. A new job, a mysterious new wand, her taboo relationship with an angel—it certainly wasn't going to be smooth sailing. But she didn't care about any of that now.

All she knew was that she was back.

And now she was a total badass!

ABOUT CATHERINE LANE

Catherine Lane started to write fiction on a dare from her wife. She's thrilled to be a published author, even though she had to admit her wife was right. They live happily in Southern California with their son and a very mischievous pound puppy.

Catherine spends most of her time these days working, mothering, or writing. But when she finds herself at loose ends, she enjoys experimenting with recipes in the kitchen, paddling on long stretches of flat water, and browsing the stacks at libraries and bookstores. Oh, and trying unsuccessfully to outwit her dog.

She has published several short stories and is currently working on a third novel.

CONNECT WITH CATHERINE:
Website: www.catherinelanefiction.wordpress.com
Facebook: www.facebook.com/CatherineLaneAuthor
E-Mail: claneauthor01@gmail.com

OTHER BOOKS FROM
YLVA PUBLISHING

HEARTWOOD

Catherine Lane

ISBN: 978-3-95533-674-5
Length: 311 pages (86,000 words)

When the law firm she works for sends Nikka to the Springs, home of lesbian author Beth Walker, she is determined to prove herself to her boss, Lea.

But nothing is as it seems. Beth is hiding her past with a film star. Lea may be keeping Beth prisoner in her own home. The only person who knows the truth is adorably impulsive Maggie.

Will Nikka dare look into the mystery—and into her own heart?

THE BUREAU OF HOLIDAY AFFAIRS
(Twice Told Tales. Lesbian Retellings – Book 3)

Andi Marquette

ISBN: 978-3-95533-549-6
Length: 289 pages (77,000 words)

Corporate executive Robin Preston didn't get where she is by being nice. That's why the Bureau of Holiday Affairs has scheduled an intervention for her that'll take her to her past, present, and future in hopes she'll be able to change her ways and open her heart to the one woman Robin thought she'd left in her past. Will the Bureau's agents succeed in their mission? Or is Robin a lost cause?

EX-WIVES OF DRACULA

Georgette Kaplan

ISBN: 978-3-95533-410-9
Length: 338 pages (122,000 words)

Mindy's best friend, Lucia, is a vampire. Every second Mindy spends with her she's in danger of becoming dinner. But Lucia needs help. To keep her alive they need fresh blood, and to cure her they have to kill her sire. So why is it that Nosferatu, the cops, and the chance of becoming an unwilling blood donor don't scare Mindy half as much as the way she feels when Lucia looks at her?

GOOD ENOUGH TO EAT
(The Vampire Diet Series – Book 1)

Jae & Alison Grey

ISBN: 978-3-95533-242-6
Length: 223 pages (64,000 words)

Robin is a vampire who wants to change her eating habits. To fight her cravings for O negative, she goes to an AA meeting, where she meets Alana, who battles her own demons.

Despite their determination not to get involved, the attraction is undeniable.

Is it love or just bloodlust that makes Robin think Alana looks good enough to eat? Will it even matter once Alana finds out who Robin really is?

COMING FROM YLVA PUBLISHING

www.ylva-publishing.com

YOU'RE FIRED

Shaya Crabtree

When an inappropriate Secret Santa gift backfires, Rose needs her smarts to save her job, while Vivian, her sexy boss, needs her smarts to save the business. Can they stop bickering long enough to do a deal?

WENDY OF THE WALLOPS
(The Wallops Series – Book 2)

Gill McKnight

These are exciting times for Community police officer Wendy Goodall. The National Crime Agency is protecting a witness in the Wallops. She has a mad crush on the reclusive Dr. Lea James. And deep suspicions concerning the new Girl Guide leader, Kiera Minsk. And together with her twin brother Will, she has to decide if she wants contact with their birth mother.

Tread Lightly
© 2017 by Catherine Lane

ISBN: 978-3-95533-817-6

Also available as e-book.

Published by Ylva Publishing, legal entity of Ylva Verlag, e.Kfr.
Ylva Verlag, e.Kfr.
Owner: Astrid Ohletz
Am Kirschgarten 2
65830 Kriftel
Germany

www.ylva-publishing.com

First edition: 2017

Credits
Edited by JoSelle Vanderhooft, Sandra Gerth, and Alissa McGowan
Proofread by Michelle Aguilar
Cover Design & Print Layout by Streetlight Graphics